Barry Pain

In a Canadian Canoe

The Nine Muses Minus One, and other Stories

Barry Pain

In a Canadian Canoe
The Nine Muses Minus One, and other Stories

ISBN/EAN: 9783337209162

Printed in Europe, USA, Canada, Australia, Japan

Cover: Foto ©Andreas Hilbeck / pixelio.de

More available books at **www.hansebooks.com**

THE NINE MUSES MINUS ONE

AND OTHER STORIES

BY

BARRY PAIN

London and New York

HARPER AND BROTHERS

45, ALBEMARLE STREET, W.

1898

PREFACE.

MY thanks are due to the Editor of "The Granta" for permission to reprint "In a Canadian Canoe," "The Nine Muses Minus One," and "The Celestial Grocery." They have been carefully revised, and considerable additions have been made. The rest of the volume has not appeared before, so far as I know.

Although this book appears in a "Library of Wit and Humour," I have not tried to make it *all* witty and humorous: I wanted there to be some background. I am not sure that I have not made it *all* background.

B. P.

CLEMENT'S INN,
July 1891.

CONTENTS.

IN A CANADIAN CANOE.

I.

ON ART AND SARDINES—BUT MORE ESPECIALLY SARDINES.

THERE is no pleasanter, sweeter, healthier spot than the Backs of the Colleges.

Get into your canoe at Silver Street. Put into that canoe :—

(1) The cushions of three other boats.

(2) Two pipes, in order that one may be always cool, and tobacco.

(3) One dozen boxes of matches, in order that one box may be always handy.

(4) The spiritual part of your nature, which will not take up much room, but is useful to talk to.

But do not take another man with you. I may frankly say, my reader, that you are absolutely the only man I know who has the keen appreciativeness, the capacity for quiet meditation, the dreaminess, the listlessness, the abominable laziness, that a Canadian canoe requires.

The man who would attempt to get pace on in a

Canadian canoe probably would analyse the want of harmony in the death-song which a swan never sings—or worse than that.

The man who would try to make a Canadian canoe go where he wanted would be angry, because the inspiration of a poet does not always disappoint the expectations of a commonplace nature. You must go where the boat wants to go; and that depends upon wind and current, and on the number of other boats that run into you, and the way they do it, and the language of their occupants.

*   *   *   *   *

What a beautiful thing it is to lie at full length on the cushions, and see the sky through the trees—only the angels see the trees through the sky. My boat has taken me round to the back of Queen's, and stopped just short of that little bridge. It is all old and familiar. The fowls coo as they cooed yesterday. The same two men in the same tub have the same little joke with one another in getting under the low bridge. Farther up, there is precisely the same number of flies on the same dead and putrescent animal. My boat went up to look at it, but could not stay. The recoil sent it back here; and here, apparently, it means to stop. You may take my word for it that a Canadian canoe knows a thing or two.

I wish I could paint the song of the birds and set the beauty of the trees to music. But there is a prejudice against it. Music is masculine, Art is feminine, and Poetry is their child. The baby Poetry will play with any one; but its parents observe the division of sexes. That is why Nature is so decent and pleasant. I would treat her to some poetry if I did but know the names of things. For instance, I have no idea what that bird is, and asparagus is the only tree which I recognise at sight.

I suppose you know that Art and Music are separated now. They sometimes meet, but they never speak. In the vacation I met them both one night by the edge of the sea; but they did not notice me. Art was busy in catching the effect of the moonlight and the lights on the pier. She did it well, and made it more beautiful than the reality seemed. Music listened to the wash of the waves, the thin sound of the little pebbles drawn back into the sea, and the constant noise of a low wind. He sat at a big organ, which was hidden from my sight by dark curtains of cloud; and as he played the music of all things came out into a song which was better than all things: for Art and Music are not only imitative, but creative. At present they are allowed to create only shadows, by the rules of the game. But I have been told that the old quarrel between them—I have no conception what the quarrel was about—will be made up one day, and they will love one another again. Their younger child, who will then be born, will take unto himself the strength and beauty of Art and Music and Poetry. He will be different from all three, and his name is not fixed yet.

Oh, confound the boat! I wish I'd tied it up. It's just taken the painter between its teeth, and whipped sharp round and bolted. Woa, my lass, steady! It's a little fresh, you see, not having been out before this week. I *beg* your pardon, sir—*entirely* my fault.

I don't think he need have been so offensively rude about it. It's not as if I'd upset him.

A fish jumped.

I know not the names of fishes, but it was not salmon steak or filleted soles, of that I'm sure. My boat goes waggling its silly old bows as if it knew but would not tell me. Can it have been a sardine?

No; the sardine is a foreign fish. It comes from Sardinia, where the Great Napoleon was exiled, as likely as not. It cannot swim in fresh water, but is brought to us in tins, which are packed in crates on trucks. It comes *en huiles*, in fact. Hence the inscription.

I cannot help thinking of the sad story of those two historical sardines—a buck-sardine and a doe-sardine—that lived on opposite sides of an island, which happened to be in the Ægean Sea.

They loved one another dearly; but they never, never told their love. He had no self-confidence, and she had too much self-respect. They met but once before their last day. It was at a place of worship in the neighbourhood of the Goodwin Sands. She caught his eye, and the umpire gave it out, and he had to go out. "Am I a hymn?" he said, just a little bitterly, "that I should be given out?" He was not a hymn, but he was a he, and had a tender heart.

All day long he sat on a stone, tail uppermost, and felt his position acutely. "Ah, if she only knew!" he sighed to himself.

And she was the life and soul of a select party in the roaring Adriatic. She quipped, and quirked; she became so brilliant that the surface of the sea grew phosphorescent. And no one guessed that beneath that calm exterior the worm was gnawing at the heart of the poor doe-sardine. No one would have been so foolish. For is it not well known that when a worm and a fish meet it's mostly the fish that does the gnawing? Still, the doe-sardine did feel a trifle weary. Why might she not tell her love? Why must she suffer?

"Il faut souffrir pour être belle," as the gong said when the butler hit it.

About this time a young man, who was dancing attendance on Queen Cleopatra, happened to be passing on a P.N.O. steamer. This was in the republican era, when Duilius introduced the P.N.O. line. The Carthaginian merchants, with a keen eye for business, always used P.T.O. steamers, which were insured far beyond their value by unsuspecting offices in the less tutored parts of Spain. These wild tribes did not know what P.T.O. signified, but the steamers did ; so did the crews of low Teutonic slaves, who were thus saved all the worry and expense of burial.

But let us return to our sardines. The young man on the P.N.O. steamer was reading a novel of Ouida's ; and, misliking the book, he flung it into the ocean. The attendants of the doe-sardine brought it to their mistress, and she read it with avidity, and after that she became very elegant, and very French.

She sat in the rose-tinted boudoir, with a sad smile on her gills, dreaming of her love. "Ah !" she murmured faintly, "Si vous saviez."

She could not sleep ! No sooner had she closed her eyes than she was haunted by an awful vision of a man soldering up tins of fish. The doctors prescribed narcotics. When she had taken the morphia of the doctors she had no more fear of the dream. But she took too much of it. She took all there was of it. Then the doctors prescribed coral, and she took any amount of coral. She would have taken in a reef; but the auctioneer was away for his Easter holidays, and consequently there were no sales. So she took in washing instead. Then, and not till then, she knew that she must die.

A fishing-net was passing, and a conductor stood on the step. "'Ere yer are, lyedy!" he called out. "Hall the way—one penny! Benk, Benk, Gritty Benk!" He used to say this so quickly that he was called the lightning conductor. She entered the net, and as she did so she saw the buck-sardine seated there. She staggered, and nearly fell!

"Moind the step, lyedy," cried the conductor.

And so they were brought to the gritty bank of the Mediterranean, and received temporary accommodation without sureties or publicity—on note-of-hand simply. As they came in with the tide, they were naturally paid into the current account.

They were preserved in the same tin, and served on the same piece of buttered toast.

As the man consumed the bodies of the buck-sardine and the doe-sardine, the two spiritualities of the two fishes walked down the empyrean, and cast two shadows.

When he had gulped down the last mouthful, the two shadows melted into one.

So they found peace at last; and I do not refer to buttered toast. But the queerest part of it is that they were both sprats.

*   *   *   *   *

It has turned chilly. No one but myself is left on the river, and the solitary end of the afternoon is good to

look at. The thing that you and I want most is a power
of expression. When I say you, I mean the sympathetic
reader who can enter into the true spirit of loafing: the
loafing of the body in the wayward Canadian canoe that
does what it likes, and the loafing of the mind that does
not take the nauseous trouble to think straight. I want
the younger child who is to be born when Art and Music
are reconciled again, who will never take aim and yet
never miss the mark, who will be quite careless but quite
true. That child will know all about the sympathy which
exists between one man and one scene in which he finds
himself, and may perhaps reveal it to us.

But I am sorry for poor Art. She is a woman, and,
though her beauty will not leave her, she desires recon-
ciliation and love.

I am taken with a sudden verse or two. Kindly excuse
them :—

> O Art, that lives not in the studio,
>   That has no special love for northern light !
> Unto no studies from the nude I owe
>   Sense of my weakness, knowledge of thy might.
> And to no stippling from the good antique,
> My shame and joy before the joyous Greek.
>
>   For I have walked in galleries oftentimes,
>   And shaded with one hand a longing eye ;
>   And found no touch of love to soften times
>   As hard as nails, as dead to ecstasy ;
>   And nothing in the gallery was fair,
>   But the worn face of the commissionaire.
>
>   So in despair I wax a trifle coarse,
>   And eat a hearty steak, and drink my beer ;
>   And twenty thousand million rifle-corps
>   Of evil spirits enter in and jeer.
>   "She's dead and rotten !" cries my angry heart,
>   And sleeps—and sees the living face of Art.

II

ON EXALTATION: TOGETHER WITH AN ANECDOTE FROM THE ENTERTAINMENTS OF KAPNIDES.

ON quiet days, when no wind blows, my canoe is particularly restful. It has perfect sympathy with the weather. It creeps down slowly to King's, leans itself against the bank, and thinks. Then, later in the afternoon, it hears the organ humming in the chapel—a faint, sweet sound which produces religious exaltation; and it becomes necessary to wrestle with the canoe, because it desires to fly away and be at rest. It is owing to this rhythmic alternation of laziness and spirituality in the boat that I have given it the name which is blazoned on its bows— *Zeitgeist.*

I have said the boat has sympathy with the weather. It also has sympathy with me, or I have sympathy with it, which is the same thing. There was a time when I suffered only from rhythmic alternations of two kinds of laziness. Now exaltation is beginning to enter in as well, and I do not know the reason, unless I have caught it from the boat. Materialistic friends have told me that too much pudding will cause exaltation. I have not so much as looked upon pudding this day. An unknown poet comes swiftly past me   I hail him, and ask him for information.

He tells me that he had been that way himself, and that with him it is generally caused by the scent of gardenias, or hyacinths, or narcissus.

I am glad he has gone away. I think if he had stayed a moment longer I should have been a little rude.

Anyway, I have got it. When one suffers from it, memory-vignettes come up quickly before the mental eye, and the mental eye has a rose-tinted glass stuck in it.

O passi graviora, dabit deus his quoque finem.

That is a memory-vignette. I am back again at school in a low form, and I am asked to parse "passi," and I parse it humorously, and there is awful silence; and then one sharp click, because the master in nervous irritation snaps in two the cedar pencil in his hand. I hate him, and he hates me. For the meaning of the words I care nothing. Now I think over them again, and I see that Virgil is very intimate with me, and that he knows the way I feel.

Up comes another quotation, this time from a more modern author :—

The sun was gone now; the curled moon
  Was like a little feather
Fluttering far down the gulf; and now
  She spoke through the still weather:
Her voice was like the voice the stars
  Had when they sang together.

Yes, and if he had said that the curled moon was like a bitten biscuit thrown out of window in a high wind, it would not have been much less true. But there is no poetry in a biscuit, and precious little sustenance. The gentle fall of a feather is full of poetry :—

> The day is done, and the darkness
> Falls from the wings of night,
> As a feather is wafted downward
> From an eagle in his flight.

Edgar Allan Poe quoted those lines in his lecture on The Poetic Principle, and remarked on their insouciance. Well, he's dead.

There are no more memory-vignettes. I have no more exaltation left. For a certain young woman crossed the bridge, and she had a baby with her, and a young man behind her. And she had the impertinence to call the baby's attention to my canoe. Then she spoke winged words to the infant, and these are the exact winged words she used :—

"Chickey-chickey-chickey, boatey-boatey-boatey, o-o-m ! Do you love auntey?"

And she called to the young man, saying, "'Enry, cummere. 'Ere's a boat."

Then they staggered slowly away, and took my exaltation with them. Just as I was getting a little better, the wind set in the wrong direction, and I heard her say some of it over again.

There is magic in the words. They set a man thinking of his past, his bills, and things which he has done and wishes he had left undone. All at once it seems as if it were going to rain. The wind turns colder. The cushions of the canoe change to brickbats. Somebody nearly runs into me, and I drop my pipe, and remember I never posted that letter after all. I look at my watch, and, of course, it's stopped. Mainspring broken, probably. The way that woman talked was enough to destroy the works of a steam-engine. And I have a twinge in my side which I am quite sure is heart disease. I had not hoped for Westminster Abbey quite so soon. "Deeply lamented. No flowers, by request."

And all this is due to the fearful words which that woman spoke, or it may be merely reaction. If one gets too high, or too low, one pays for it afterwards; and the common-place praises of *aurea mediocritas* are properly founded. The quietist never pays, because he incurs no debts. All the rest pay, and there is no dun like a Natural Law. It may agree to renew for a short time, on the consideration of that small glass of brandy, perhaps, or a week's rest; but one has to pay for the accommodation, and the debt must be discharged in the end.

Do you remember that quaint old story told by Kapnides in his third book of Entertainments? Well, Kapnides is not enough read at Oxford or Cambridge. I doubt if he is read at all. He is a little artificial, perhaps, but he has his points. It is the story of a Greek boy.

No; it is not the story of the Spartan boy who lied about a fox, and subsequently died of the lies which were told about himself.

It is the story of an Athenian boy, who in the month of June sat quite alone in a thin tent by night. And the tent was pitched under the shadow of the long wall, and the night was hot and stifling.

He sat alone, for dead men are no company. His father and his eldest brother were in the tent with him; but he was alone. He had not been afraid to tend

them in their sickness, for he had himself recovered from
the pestilence; but it had taken away from him his beauty
and his memory. He had been very beautiful, and his
mind had been very full of fair memories. All were gone
now. He kept only the few bare facts which his dying
father had told him, that his mother had died long before;
that they had lived in the country and had been ordered
into the city; that Pericles had made a remarkably fine
speech in the preceding year; and that his only surviving
relation was his twin-brother, who had gone away into
Eubœa with the sheep. On these few poor facts, and on
the two dead manly bodies before him, he pondered as he
sat. And the night grew late, and yet he could hear outside the tent people passing busily, and quarrels, and long
horrible cries.

And suddenly the poor Greek boy, with the ghost of
an old beauty haunting his dull eyes and scarred cheeks,
looked up, because he was conscious of the presence of a
deity; and there before him sat an old gentleman in a silk
hat, a frock-coat worn shiny under the fore arm, pepper-
and-salt trousers, with a pen stuck at the back of his ear.

"I perceive a divine fragrance," the boy said. The
fragrance was gin-and-water, but he knew it not. "And
about thy neck there is a circle of brightness." In this
he was correct, because the old gentleman was wearing an
indiarubber dickey covered with luminous paint, which
saves washing and makes it possible to put in a stud in the
dark. "And thy dress is not like unto mine. It cannot
be but that thou art some god. And at the right time art
thou come; for my heart is heavy, and none but a god can
comfort me. And due worship have I ever rendered to

the gods, but they love me not, and they have taken all things from me; and only my twin-brother is left, and he keeps the sheep in Euboea. And what name dost thou most willingly hear?"

"Allow me," said the old gentleman, and produced a card from his pocket, handing it to the boy. On it was printed:—

THE PROLEPTICAL CASHIER.

(Agent for Zeus & Co., Specialists in Punishments.)

"The tongue is barbarian," said the boy, "and thy spoken words are barbarian, and yet I understand them; and now I know that the gods are kinder to me, because already I have greater wisdom than my fathers, and, perhaps, somewhat greater remains. Give to me, O cashier, the power to stay this pestilence."

"For a young 'un," said the cashier, "that's pretty calm, seeing that I *made* that pestilence. I just want to go into your little account. Your great-grandpapa, my boy, incurred a little debt, and Zeus & Co. want the thing settled before they dissolve partnership. They've just taken those two lives." He touched the body of the boy's father lightly with his foot. "They've taken your beauty and your memory. How sweet the girls used to be on you, my lad! but you can't recollect it, and you won't experience it again. You *are* a bad sight. Now we shall just kill your brother, and give the sheep the rot, and then the thing will be square. Now then, it's a hot night, and you'd better burn these two. I'll show you how to do it on the cheap, without paying for it. As long as Zeus & Co. are paid I don't care about the rest."

The boy sat dazed, and did not speak.

"There's a rich man built a first-class pyre twenty yards from your tent. They've gone to fetch his dead daughter to burn on it. We'll collar it before they get back. I'll take the old man, because he's the lightest. You carry your brother. He was a hoplite, wasn't he, one of them gentlemen that do parasangs? Oh, I know all about it."

Still the boy did not speak. They took up the two bodies, passed out of the tent, and laid their burden on the pyre.

"You look as if something had hurt you," said the old gentleman. "I like these shavings miles better than newspaper." He pulled a box of matches from his pocket, and set light to the pyre. It flared up brightly.

Then the boy touched him on the shoulder, and pointed first in the direction of Eubœa, and then at himself. A word came into him from a future civilisation.

"Swop?" he said gently.

"All right," grumbled the cashier. "I don't mind. It gives a lot of trouble—altering the books. But I don't mind, I'm sure. It's a thirsty night."

For a moment the boy stood motionless; then, with a little cry, leapt into the flames. And his life went to join his beauty and his memory in a land of which we know too little.

*   *   *   *   *

It's begun to rain. I think I'll be off. I do hate anachronisms.

III.

ON SELF-DECEPTION : TOGETHER WITH THE DREAM OF THE DEAN'S PREPARATIONS.

THIS morning, because the air was fresh, and the sun was bright, and I had eaten too much breakfast, it seemed to be an excellent thing to cut all lectures and to loaf in the Backs. Few boats are there in the morning, and I have found, when my canoe takes me out, that the fewer the boats the less the unpleasantness. I can run into a bridge, but a bridge cannot run into me; and a bridge always takes my apologies in a nice spirit. The afternoon loafers on the river are not yet sufficiently educated to understand that a Canadian canoe must go its own way, and that any attempt to control it is a baseness.

The other afternoon my canoe got a little humorous. It saw a man on in front of us working hard in one of those vessels that went a thousand miles down the Jordan —or something to that effect. I knew what my canoe would do. It broke into a canter, caught the absolute stranger in the back of the neck, and knocked him into the water. You would have expected the absolute stranger to have come up, breathing the Englishman's Shortest Prayer. He did not. He apologised for having been in my way, said that it was entirely his own fault, and hoped that he

had not inconvenienced me.   I shrugged my shoulders and
forgave him, with considerable hauteur.

But my boat got Remorse badly.   It did not want to
live any more, and tried to knock its brains out against
Clare Bridge.   I soothed it, and tied it up.   Canadian
canoes are such sensitive things.

This sort of incident cannot happen when one cuts
lectures to go on the river in the morning.   And one does
more work.   You take your Plato's "Phædo," and you
really enjoy it.   If there's any word you don't know, you
leave it; if there's any sentence you can't understand,
you don't worry about it; and if there's any word you *can*
understand, it goes home to you more.   That's the right
spirit.   That's the way the ancient Greeks took their
language.   What did they know about dictionaries and
grammars and cribs?   And then, after a couple of minutes,
one pitches the "Phædo" into the bows of the boat, and
a great Peace falls on one's soul.

My Better Self does not agree with me on these points;
but I had words with my Better Self this morning, and
since then we have not been on speaking terms.   I find
it impossible to convince my Better Self of great truths;
I could deceive my Better Self, which is a common practice,
but I will not do it.   I have seen men do it; and I have
been very, very sorry for them.   I have known a man, who
had previously been honest, commence to keep an average
of the amount of work he did *per diem*.   The way he faked
that average would have brought a blush to the cheek of
the chartered libertine, and made the chartered accountant
moan for humanity.   The first week gave a daily average
of 2 hours 20·5 minutes.   In the second week we were

asked to believe that he had done rather more than ten hours a day. That man drives a cab now: self-deception never pays. Another man, who was quite a friend of mine, liked pork chops. He pretended that he didn't, and made himself believe that he didn't. Why? Simply and solely because he once wrote a poem—and published it—which began :

Darling, thy hot kiss lingers on my lips.

Before he wrote that poem, he used to feed almost entirely on pork chops. After it was published, he pretended that a little ripe fruit was all he needed. What's become of him? What do you suppose? Trichinosis, of course. It's much better to be perfectly honest. The worst case of all was last May. A man made himself believe that he loved Bradelby's sister, and he never got any better. He just pined away and married her. Perhaps you don't realise what that means, but you never met Bradelby's sister.

I met her. She sat down at the piano, and stroked it as if it were a lap-dog. She was quite tender in her movements, and she sang :

Once in the deeeeer dead dyes beyond recall.

Shortly afterwards she said that she wanted to live a useful life. That sort of thing stamps a woman.

* * * * *

I suppose I must have been going to sleep when I thought that last sentence. For I suddenly found myself in the centre of Epping Forest, and before me was a college dean in full academicals. He was a leathery old dean to look at, and yet he had some nervousness of manner. Of course he was not a real dean, but only a dream dean. The real deans—I cannot say it too emphatically—are *not* leathery, and are *not* nervous.

When he saw me, he began to rub his hands gently and to smile, until I thought my heart would break.

"This is a little unusual," he said; "a little irregular, is it not? Have you permission, may I ask, from the University authorities, to drive a Canadian canoe tandem through Epping Forest?"

"No, sir," I said politely; "but I was not aware that permission was required."

"Epps's Forest," he retorted inanely, "contains absolutely no fatty matter. Applicants are therefore assured, if they cannot borrow here, it would be futile to apply elsewhere. Personal visit invited."

"But, sir," I urged, "this is a personal——"

"Stop!" he interrupted me, tapping the palm of one hand with the forefinger of the other. "That's not the point, and you know it's not the point. I have come here to practise my part—Titania—in *Midsummer Night s Dream*, with real fairies. I do not do it because I like it. I do it because I wish to entertain and interest some young ladies who will be staying with me during the June festivities. You interrupt my preparations, you frighten the fairies, you annoy me exceedingly, and your attendance in college chapel is not what it should be. You've been smoking, and you smell. Where no allotment is made the deposit will be returned in full."

I could not quite make it out, because the dean did not seem as if he would make up into a good Titania. But that was the only thing that surprised me. I promised to sit quite still, and not to frighten the fairies, and entreated him to go on with the rehearsal.

"Very well," he said, seating himself on a camp-stool. "You will not see the fairies; but you will hear them. We are now commencing Act II., Scene iii. I give them their cue :—

> Sing me now asleep ;
> Then to your offices, and let me rest.

Now, then they sing—

> You spotted snakes with double tongue.

You know it?"

I knew it very well; but what the fairies really sang was this :—

FIRST FAIRY.

> You potted slates, disguised as tongue,
>   Cornèd oxen be not seen ;
> Such things never put him wrong,
>   Never hurt the college dean.

CHORUS.

> Fill him up with mayonnaise,
> Made in several different ways ;
> (Salmon, chicken mayonnaise ; also lobster mayonnaise) ;
>   Never fear,
>   'Twill keep him queer,
> Shocking queer for several days ;
> He *can't* work on mayonnaise.

SECOND FAIRY.

> Curried rabbits, come not nigh ;
>   Hence, tomato-tinners, hence !
> He can eat what you or I
>   Wouldn't for a hundred pence.

(Chorus as before.)

"There," exclaimed the dean, turning to me, "that goes pretty well, I think. Shakespeare would be pleased. I shall play *Midsummer Night's Dream* on the first night of the visit of my lady friends. On the second night I am going to sing themsome songs. On the third night I shall give a conjuring entertainment." He suddenly stopped, and burst into tears. "And on the fourth night," he sobbed, "their funeral will take place, and they are so young and fair!"

"Couldn't you fix their funeral for the first night?" I asked. "They'd suffer less so."

"No," said the dean firmly, "they must be amused first —amused and interested and entertained. And I must amuse them, and I never amused any one in my life before. I can't take them to the races, because there are undergraduates about. I can't take them to dances for similar reasons. I'm going to do it all myself." He burst out sobbing again. "And I know it will kill them. The fairies won't play out of Epping Cocoa, so I shall have to undertake every character in the piece. Now I must go back, and practise my songs. I am *so* anxious to be amusing. It quite weighs on my mind. You don't know anything that would do for the conjuring entertainment, do you? Card-tricks, you know, or think-of-any-number-you-like, or something of that sort?"

As he said these words he got into my boat, which started down a river that flowed into a drawing-room. We got out. Then the boat changed into a piano, and the dean sat down to it, and began to play the symphony.

"It's one of those simple, touching songs, and it's called 'Papa.'"

Then he sang :

> Take my head on your shoulders, papa,
>   Let's have it back when you've done ;
> I only unscrewed it in jest, papa—
>   Only unscrewed it in fun.
> And it's pleasant to lie and to think, papa,
>   You can give it me back all right ;
> My head, though it's screwed, is loose, papa,
>   And you, when you're screwed, are tight.

" You can't possibly sing that to the ladies," I said.

" No," he answered ; " I've kept the words a little too long, and the weather's been hot. I'll try another—a fervent and passionate one."

" No, you won't," I said firmly, and jumped into the piano, which changed into the canoe again, and started away down the river.

" That's the wrong 'bus !" the dean shrieked after me. He shrieked so loudly that he woke me. At least, he half woke me. I was so full of the idea that I was in the wrong 'bus that I got out. The canoe was in the middle of the river at the time. You will find an excellent edition of Plato's " Phædo," a copy of last week's *Review*, and my nicest pipe at the bottom of the river in King's. At any rate, you may go and dive for them if you like.

IV

ON REFLECTION; TO WHICH IS ADDED THE STORY OF
THE TIN HEART.

I LIKE to watch those trees reflected in the water. They are so suggestive, by reason of their being reflected wrong way up. All objective, outside facts are as trees, and the mind of man is as a river, and he consequently reflects everything in an inverted way. That is the reason why, if I try to guess a coin and say heads, it is always tails. That is the reason why, if I go to get a spoon out of my plate-basket in the dark, I always take out thirteen successive forks before I find one. It explains nearly everything. Probably the correct way to dine is really to begin with the fruit and end with the oysters. Itinerant musicians should begin by making a collection and leave out the other part. Anything that *can* be done backwards is better done backwards. When I leave for a moment the presence of royalty I am always required to walk backwards. That shows that royalty, together with Her Privy Council, which is the collected wisdom of the nation, thinks that it is best to walk backwards. And so it is. It is not only happier and holier, but it is also more piquant. You can never tell until you've kicked it whether you have backed into a policeman or a lamp-post. New possibilities are open to you. Anything may happen, and generally does. So, too, in skating. A good skater told me that the only enjoyable method of progression is the outside edge backwards. "It makes you feel like a bird," he said; "and I don't believe you can get that sensation of flight any other way." He simply seemed to float on the ice. You see, he was a good skater. At last he galumphed into a snow-heap, flew just like a bird for a few yards, then came down hard and hurt a lady. Look at these railway collisions, too. We all know what an awful thing a railway collision is : and how does it always happen? It happens from two trains wanting to go to the same spot and arriving there simultaneously. If both trains had respectively reversed their directions, no collision could have happened. A train should never be allowed to *go* anywhere, but only to *back* to the place whence it came. But, as I should like these pages to be of solid, material use to any young men who are really trying to lead the philosophical life, and are quite earnest in their desire to avoid the Scylla of action without falling into the Charybdis of thought, I will put my facts and deductions clearly and briefly. The facts are two :—

(1) That a tree is reflected in the water wrong way up.

(2) That the reflection of such a reflection would be right way up.

From No. 2 we deduce that the best literary method is to crib some other man's ideas or reflections; and this is what I always do when I write an article.

From No. 1 we deduce that as all reflection is the reverse of the thing reflected, it is best to act altogether without reflection ; and this is what the editor always does when he prints my articles ; and what you yourselves do when you pay two-and-sixpence for this volume in spite of it.

In the meanwhile, my dear old sympathetic canoe has been going slowly backwards on its own account, and must be stopped.

* • • • •

It was only the other night that I took my canoe out in the moonlight, when the river is solitary and quiet. I shall not take it by night any more, because it is too sympathetic. A man came and leaned over one of the bridges and watched the reflection of the spangled skies in the ripple. He sighed, and said, " Prec lil starsh ! " Then he swore hard at them. Then he sighed again, and his cap tumbled off into the water. "Ish all over now," he said solemnly, and walked wearily away. My boat simply shuddered. I could feel it shudder.

After that it got absurdly sentimental. Now I hate and I despise sentiment. I suppose it was the effect of the moonlight. It made some verses. At least I suppose the boat made them. I found them in my blazer pocket afterwards, and I'm sure I recognised the handwriting. So I will give them in full. (You will do nothing of the kind.—Ed.)

I'm not going to discuss the merit of those verses. There may be something in them which the world will one day learn to cherish, or there may not be ; but I deprecate the weakness and sentimentality which cause verse. We want to be strong, really strong. We want more of the spirit of that Gallic chieftain who wanted a tin heart made for himself. The story is well enough known, and you will find it in Livy : it is in one of the lost books ; but I give it for the benefit of readers who are not classical. I do not scorn such readers. I can remember the time when I had not the finished scholarship, the critical insight, the almost insolent familiarity with the more recondite parts of history, which—with all modesty be it spoken—I know that I now possess.

I have forgotten some of the names, all the dates, and a few of the facts. But these are not the essentials. Such things are but the dry bones of history. We want the flesh and blood and sinews—the words, the large, beautiful, vague words that smudge over a difficulty until you can't see it.

To understand why the Gallic chieftain wanted a tin heart, we must first of all appreciate the man's character.

When the Gallic tribe, to which he belonged, formed one of their sudden plans (*Gallorum subita sunt consilia*), he was always in the front of the battle; but when he was at home he used to smoke his pipe in the back yard, because his wife and her mother would not allow it in the house. He had plenty of fighting courage, but no domestic courage. And there were other points in which he saw that he was weak. Sometimes, for instance, he found some aged veteran in the streets, in a state of destitution, with a card on his breast to say that he had lost his wife in a colliery explosion, selling *sulfura*, or playing on the *tuba telescopica*, an instrument resembling the trombone, but more deleterious. Whenever this happened, he would buy the matches, or give the man money. It was weak of him, but he couldn't help it.

The tribe to which he belonged was transcendental, heterodox, habitually untruthful, and characterised by a belief that the affections resided in the heart. So, when this poor chieftain found that he was getting too good and kind (ah, how many of us have felt like that!—I often have), he concluded that something must be wrong with his heart, and went to a medicine man or *fakir*. And he said: " O fakir, would you fake me up a tin heart? For the heart which I have is too unpleasantly soft, and I want a metal one." The fakir agreed to make the change for twelve ducats. But just at this time an accident happened to the budget of this tribe, and a tax of ten ducats per pound was put on *plumbum album*—no, my boy, not white lead: it means tin. So it was quite clear to the fakir that he could not afford to give the man a tin heart, and yet he had signed the document. Besides, he wanted those twelve ducats.

So he gave the man chloroform, removed his heart, and then proceeded to do his best with a cheap substitute. But the cheap substitute refused to be faked, and the fakir was still hard at work trying to make something which should do quite as well as a tin heart and last longer, when he noticed signs of reviving consciousness in the chieftain. He had no more chloroform to give him, and no time to lose. So he hurriedly sewed up the incision, and left the man with no heart at all, neither of flesh, nor of tin, nor of cheap substitute.

Then the chieftain started off home, and he looked very cheerful indeed. He tripped up two blind men, and threw their *sulfura* down a grating. Then he went into a public-house, and spent his week's *stipendium*. Finally, he reeled home, kicked his wife, smoked two cigars in the drawing-room, broke his mother-in-law's head, forgot to wipe his boots, said he wanted some tea, and went to sleep with his feet on the crimson plush mantelpiece.

Now, next day another Gaul was going down the street when he saw two goats being harnessed to a milk-cart. It at once occurred to him that it would be as well to throw off the Roman yoke. So another insurrection was started, and the Gallic chieftain who had no heart was put in the forefront of the battle.

Just as the trumpets sounded for a charge, this Gallic chieftain remembered that he had left his handkerchief in the tent, and went to look for it in a hurry, and got himself disliked. But as the rest of the tribe were mostly killed in the charge, he did not mind that much. The survivors said : " Our noble chief has begun to be a coward." But he was not afraid of his wife, and used bad language in her presence during mealtimes. One of the survivors went so far as to run a lance through the place where the chieftain's heart ought to have been. The chieftain smiled, and said sarcastically that he was not an umbrella-stand.

Death is connected with the stoppage of the heart's action; consequently this chieftain never died, and it is argued that during the Syro-Phœnician attempt to——

* * * * *

Here there is a hiatus in the manuscript. A scribe has added a note in the margin *pallido atramento*, " The chieftain is still alive. I have seen him. I have written his name at the foot of the manuscript." I have looked there, and simply found the words " *Venditus iterum.*"

But the other day I bought a cigar which was all case and no inwards. The tobacconist who sold it me said it was a Regalia Gallica ; and he looked as if he had been in this world a long time, and had seen the wickedness of it. I simply mention this as a coincidence. There may be nothing in it, like the cigar. But it is a curious case, if nothing else—also like the cigar.

V.

A STORM ON THE BACKS; AND A STORY OF THREE.

I HAVE often considered it as one of my misfortunes that I simply do not know what fear is. As a boy I was so brave and bright that every one loved me; in my manhood my courage appals me. I feel that one day it will carry me too far.

As I climbed hand-over-hand up the side of the *Zeitgeist* at the Silver Street Docks, an old, old sailor stepped up to me. "Young stranger," he said, "you will not attempt to make King's Bridge on such a day as this? It would be madness. The boldest of us dare not."

"Avaunt!" I cried; "where honour calls I follow. England expects. *Per ardua ad astra.*"

He turned away to hide his emotion. I gave him my hand, which he wrung and knocked twice. There was no answer.

With one wild, exultant leap the vessel burst from its moorings, churning the iron-bound waves to sheer desperation, foaming at the mouth, and sobbing piteously. Through the driving rain, the blinding fog, the dazzling lightning, the impenetrable mist, and the other atmospheric phenomena which Mr. Clark Russell had lent for the occasion, loomed a hideous dark object. I consulted the chart, the compass, the telescope, the ship's biscuits, every-thing I could lay my hands on ; but it was too late. Nearer and nearer it loomed. I could see that it was Silver Street Bridge, *and that it was coming my way.* Oh, the horror of it !

I shrieked to it to save itself and go away. But my voice was drowned in the fury of the elements. It loomed nearer —it never stopped looming once—and I knew that I should be unable to avoid it, that I should destroy it.

Bump ! From the top of the bridge there came the voice of a small boy, asking if I was insured. He seemed hysterical, and fear had probably sapped his reason. I was swept on by the fury of the elements. No, I've just had that—swept on by the elemental fury—well, that's much the same.

At any rate, I was swept on. The wind whistled in the rigging, until it got sick of being conventional. Then it went and whistled in the taffrail. At last it got so nastily original that it sang " Since first I saw your Face " in the binnacle. A hasty glance backward showed me that Silver Street Bridge was yet standing. My resolution was also unshaken.

The fierce old Berserker spirit fired my blood. Chanting aloud the grand old Latin hymn of the Crusaders—

A, ab, absque, coram, de,
Palam, clam, cum, ex and e—

I dashed forward. My speed may be guessed from the fact that by this time I was under Queen's Bridge. Before me, or close behind me, or at any rate on one side or the other, lowered in thick banks of cloud an angry sun, red as the blood of an orange that the thunder had pealed! The waves were mountain high.

The light of the unbroken Viking was in my eyes. I could not see them, but I knew that it must be so. The waves were mounting higher now.

Suddenly the wind shifted. It became semicircular, with a pendulum action. It swung my boat round to the left, then swung it round to the right. It kept on doing this. A horrible thought flashed across me that I should never make King's Bridge at this rate. I said "Excelsior" to the boat to encourage it, but it only went on wagging. I smote it on the bows with the flat of my paddle, and that had no effect. Lastly, I raised myself about four inches, and sat down again with the energy and directness of the wild Norsemen. The jerk started it on again. We went so fast that a sparrow seemed to be literally flying past me. I believe that was what it actually *was* doing. By this time the waves were quite extraordinary.

We were now but a few yards from home. There was another change in the weather. The sun was like a crystal chalice brimming with crimson wine, borne by an unseen Ganymede to his lord across the sapphire pavement of cloud. (Poetry is cheap to-day.) Had his white feet slipped on the wondrous far-off way? For of a sudden the crimson flood suffused the sapphire floor, and the gasp of the dying wind was as of one who cried, "Come away in my 'and, sir, and it was cracked before, and you didn't ought to have left it there, and I never touched it, and 'ow was I to know yer didn't want it broke?" Then the wind sank. My boat was motionless. I was becalmed within sight of my goal.

So I waited in the middle of the river. The storm was passed, and the waves were perfectly calm and collected, like a bad halfpenny in an offertory bag. There was not a breath of wind, and consequently the first two matches which I lit were blown out at once. The third match did what was expected of it, and then I attempted to blow *it* out. Finding this impossible, I threw it in the water. It floated on the top, and burnt with a clear steady flame for ten consecutive minutes. While I was watching it I let my pipe out, and had to strike a fourth match. The head came off it, and nestled lovingly in the palm of my hand. Then it walked away, and burned two holes in my blazer. How such little incidents as this make one wish that the nature of things was otherwise!

I may own that I never did make King's Bridge that afternoon. My canoe did not seem to care about going there of its own accord, and I did not like to paddle it there because I hate unnecessary fuss; so I just stopped where I was and read a little.

What was I reading?

Well, I had his book, you know, after his death. Some of it interests me; but this is chiefly because I knew the man. He wrote it as a remedy, and he died as a remedy; but I have a notion that he is not quite cured yet. I take the book here to read sometimes. You may see a page or two of it. I am not pretending that it has any literary value But try to think you knew the man who wrote it.

*   *   *   *   *

She shivered a little as she sat there in her nightdress. In the small hours of the morning in early summer it is always cold. She would have been much warmer in bed; she really ought to have been in bed; but the bed had not been slept in. It stood there in one corner of the room, looking white and restful. It seemed to be calling her, "Come to me; sleep and forget it—sleep and forget it." On the little table at the foot of the bed was the pile of books and newspapers that had slowly accumulated. She had always been interested in the world and in the things others did and thought.

A little impulse that came to her from nowhere made her pick up the newspaper that lay on the top of the pile. It would do to fill her mind and to keep her thoughts steady until the morning came. Her eyes ached, and the candles flickered on the dressing-table. Her brain seemed to her as a pool into which some thoughtless child that did what he liked had flung a stone, starting circle after circle, circles that grew and grew, spreading to the farther edge, and sobbing away into nothing because they could go no farther. Yet she read, and knew nothing of what she read, till one sentence seemed to shine brighter than the rest.

"The body had probably been in the water for several days."

She stood up quickly, with a little gasp, and let the newspaper fall to the ground. For her brain, burning with torture and want of sleep, had suddenly flashed out a merciless, truthful, coloured illustration to that sentence. She steadied herself in a moment. Then she held up her hands and looked at them. "Will they turn like that?" she was asking herself. She shivered, and the muscles of her face contracted a little

She was bending now over the mantelpiece. Her arms and her burning forehead rested upon it, and her thoughts went stealing away through the passages and rooms of the quiet old house. In the room next to hers slept stolid respectability. She loved him and her, as the accident of parentage makes love. But she must leave them. How she hated to hurt those two, those kind, misunderstanding parents, with their old ideas, and their love for her ever fresh! No, she could not leave them, she could not leave them. "You will leave them at dawn," said the thing that was stronger than herself.

And her thoughts stood mutely listening outside the door of the room where Claud lay. "Are you asleep?" she whispered. Or was he lying awake and thinking, as she thought, of the night before? It all came back to her so easily,—the wistful refrain that lingered softly on the strings, the brilliant lights and the brilliant crowd, and suddenly the dim garden outside the ball-room. She could see him standing there; she could hear him speaking. No, she could never, never leave him. "You will leave him at dawn," said the thing that was stronger than herself.

And the dawn had come now.

She drew up the blind, and opened the window softly. The sky was one dull grey but for the beauty in the east. A fresh, cool wind had awakened; and she could hear the chirrup, chirrup of waking birds. And she looked down the valley and saw the hurrying, winding river, with the grey mists hovering upon it. "River," she said in a whisper, "take me to the sea. Take me to a sea that has no shores, that will flow for ever, bearing me farther and farther away from this."

She crept down the stairs, barefooted, and into the drawing-room. She drew back the heavy curtains from the windows that opened down to the ground. Outside was the terraced garden that sloped down to the edge of the river. Her hand was on the bolt of the window.

Suddenly she heard quick footsteps coming down the passage. In a moment she had hidden herself behind the screen that stood against the door. She knew those footsteps. Involuntarily her hands linked tightly together, and her breath came quickly.

He was not so careful as she had been; he came boldly into the room, opened the window noisily, and went out into the garden. As he went out she caught one glimpse of his face, and she knew what he would do. She sprang from behind the screen. "Claud, Claud!" she called. He stopped with a sudden start, and came towards her. "What are you doing here?" he asked, in a voice that was not like his voice.

"I," she panted—"I came to save you, Claud. Oh, go back again!"

He would have taken her hands, but she shrank away from him. They only stayed there for a few minutes. She talked to him and pleaded with him. There was little need for such pleading, for he had yielded to her from the first. He gave her the only promise that she would let him make, and then he went back to his room.

She quietly closed the windows, and drew the curtains again. She seemed to herself both sad and happy now, and very tired.

And Fate had an approving smile upon her bitter face. "They are two obedient children," she said. "They were

going to take matters into their own hands, and they re-
sisted the temptation.   Very well, they shall be rewarded."

So Fate sent the girl a present of a beautiful brain-fever
with pictures in it.   And when it was over she fell asleep,
and dreamed that she was floating on a sea that had no
shores and flowed for ever, bearing her farther and farther
away from this.   And she woke no more.

And Fate thought that she should then do something
for Claud.   So she killed another woman, and killed her
with thirty other people in a railway accident, thereby
escaping any charge of impartial justice.   They both had
loved him, and they were both dead, and he got much
happier.   In the unprepared passages of this life a glimpse
at the context would be useful.

   *   *   *   *   *

Poor stuff—isn't it ?

VI.

I TOOK my canoe the other day up that part of the river where only Masters of Arts are allowed to drown themselves without a certificate. None of them were doing it on the day I was there, and it was rather dull, and the boat went to sleep with its cold nose resting on the soft grass that edged the river.

So I just stopped there and lazed, and watched other boats go past. There is a prevalent notion apparently that nothing which is said in one boat can possibly be heard in another. As each boat went past, its occupants made humorous and uncomplimentary remarks upon me. The waiters in some of the inferior London restaurants have a similar notion that nobody understands French. Without these little delusions we should not be as happy as we are. In my case there seemed to be an idea that I had got stuck in the bank and couldn't get out again. The impression was wrong. My boat was a little tired, and went to sleep. It had come a long way, and I was not brute enough to wake it up again.

I watched the other boats go past. There were very fine and noble people in some of them, but I did not see one

proper loafer, and hardly any one who had elementary
notions of the right way to loaf. There is no subject which
is less understood. The spirit of asceticism, the spirit of
extravagance for its own sake, and the spirit of utilitarianism
are fast spoiling us.

The popular idea that loafing is in some way connected
with laziness should be removed. Loafing is the science
of living without trouble. There may be a time when it
is easier to work than to laze. A man, when suffering
badly from Tripos, may find it less trouble to read Thucy-
dides than to stifle his conscience. The condition of mind
is unhealthy and morbid; but, where it exists, it would
certainly be better loafing to work than to laze. And no
one objects more than the well-trained loafer to enforced
laziness. When he is in London he will have his hat
ironed at the barber's rather than at the maker's. In the
first case he will have to pay for it, but he will be shaved
while it is being done; in the second case no charge is
made, but more than sixpennyworth of vitality is consumed
in the irritation of having to wait. It is not the waiting
which the loafer minds: it is the *having* to wait.

There are many who would loaf, but fail from want
of a little thought. They do not take enough trouble to
avoid trouble. They arrive at some result, and half a loaf
is better than no bread; but nevertheless they do not get
the perfect life.

Here is a problem in loafing.

There were four men—A, B, C, D—who rose one
morning, and all found they wanted shaving.

A was too lazy, left his chin as it was, was miserable
all that day, and simply *had* to shave next day.

B half-way through the morning got shaved at a barber's.

C conquered his inclinations and shaved himself at once.

D, knowing that it was impossible to grow a beard at Cambridge, and being too lazy to shave or be shaved, had his things packed up, and "went down."

The vanity of the man, the strength of the beard, and the distance from a barber are the same in each case ; and it is supposed that the price of a shave is so small that it may be disregarded: which was the best loafer of the four ?

There was not a perfect loafer among them, but the best was undoubtedly C, and the next best was D. This will seem strange to any one who has not studied the effect of anticipation on happiness and the reverse. Nothing is real to us except our imagination of it. What would the perfect loafer have done? I know; and you, my sympathetic reader, know. But I do not think any of the others do. And it would be of no use to tell them, because they would not believe it. The answer is too long and elaborate to be given in any case.

It should be remembered that loafing is not the science of living for pleasure, which is foolishness, but the science of living without trouble. We may believe, as it is said in "The New Republic," that one of the two most lasting pleasures is the pleasure of saying a neat thing neatly ; yet the perfect loafer will never become a conversationalist.

But it is of little use to preach. After all I have said about the quantity of cushions necessary for comfort in a Canadian canoe, I constantly see men going out with far

too few. I am always hearing complaints that we are not
taught engineering or some other horribly useful thing.
But why are we not taught the art of perfect living, which
is loafing?

    *   *   *   *   *

Only a few out of my many books do I ever bring on the
water. Some of the best would seem quite out of place.
To-day I've got that curious old translation of he " Entertainments of Kapnides " with me. I was reminded of it by
seeing those children going along in the meadow, picking
flowers. Of course you know the story well enough, but I
cannot be bothered to be original in every chapter. It is
the story of the Child Siren.

Ligeia never cared about the child from the first. It
interfered with business. It absolutely refused to play her
accompaniments, and said it could not bear to see the
sailors tempted to their death. On this particular day it
had interrupted Ligeia just as she reached the most tender,
pathetic, touching part of her song. The sob of the child
broke into the sloppy waltz refrain, and spoiled the spell.
And the helmsman had turned the ship's prow out again
from the coast, and there was another crew gone.

" You sinful little beast," said Ligeia. " Get out of my
sight."

The child was not sorry to go. She climbed up the cliff,
and then wandered on away from the sea, where the long
grass came up to her waist. And as she wandered, the sun
shone brightly, and the cool wind blew into her hair, and
the birds sang above her, and only a little distance away
sounded the drowsy murmurs of the waves.

And then for the first time in her life the passion for

song came into her. She felt that she *must* sing. Always before she had shuddered at the thought of song, for the song of Ligeia and others had ever brought death with it. But now she felt that she *must* sing, and she knew not why; for a study of hereditary tendencies was not included in the Board School education of that period. She had reached an open space now. The ground was sandy, with here and there a stunted clump of grass, and in one place a beautiful golden poppy.

"No one will hear me," she thought, "and if I do not sing my heart will break." So she sang, standing there white and naked, with the sunlight upon her, holding a lyre in her little hands.

And the music came out of her soul, but she knew not whence the words came.

She sang that it was not sweet for the golden poppy to bloom there alone, though the sun made it warm, and the wind was fragrant about it. It was sweeter that she should pluck it in her little hands, which were warm with a better life than the life of the sun, and more fragrant than the west wind with its burden of the breath of the flowers. She paused, and her fingers rested lightly on the lyre. Her eyes were strained in looking up to the east, and she did not see that the poppy had bowed its golden head and withered away.

"And it is not sweet," she sang again, "for you, white bird, to fly on and on, and never to rest. It is better to lie here, and let me touch you, and fondle you, and love you."

And out from the eastern sky flew the white bird, and it nestled for one moment at the child's breast, and then fell dead on the sand.

And the child saw what she had done, and she flung herself down beside the dead bird and the withered flower, and sobbed in the foolishest way.

So the afternoon wore on, and the sea still murmured, and she still lay there. And when it was evening a new wind sprang up from the south, and it whispered to her,—

" A girl's voice for a bird's life."

She stood up, erect, with eyes that flashed brightly, though the tears still stood in them. She held the white bird in her little hands. " I'll give you my voice," she said, as she kissed it. And the bird flew far away from her, and the girl was dumb.

For a little while she stood there, and the old passion of song came back to her, and tore at her heart; but she could not sing, for she was dumb.

" And I have nothing else left," she thought, " with which I may give back the life to the golden poppy."

" Crimson for golden," the south wind called softly in her ear.

So she lay down once more, and put her pretty mouth to the dead bloom of the poppy, and she could not speak, but she thought the words—" Drink my blood! Drink my life, and live!"

And the dead flower drained out her life, and she grew white and whiter, and when the moonlight fell upon her, not a tint of colour was in her cheeks.

Out of the forest the south wind crept, and he seemed a little excited as he saw the dead girl lying there.

" I'll never do it again," he swore; " if they want such things done, they must do them themselves. Curse them!" Then he howled, for his masters had overheard him and chastised him.

He went back to the forest, and brooded all day over what had happened. And that night he went mad, and came forth to do one or two things on his own account. There was the tall poppy growing by the head of the dead girl, and it had become crimson.

The south wind gave one puff, and blew it out of the ground into the sea.

And over the child's body it blew the finest white sand that it could find, until a heavy drift lay over it.

And it went away to a lonely place where a solitary tree was standing, and in the tree sat the white bird in her nest. And he blew down the tree, and broke the nest, and chased the bird for days and days over the water, till at last the bird sank.

And still the wind was not satisfied. He had a faint idea that he had not been doing much good. He ought, by rights, to have killed his masters. He knew that, but his masters could not be killed. How they smiled as they sat up in cloudland, and watched their angry servant snarling over a child, a bird, and a flower! "He's not satisfied," said the first. "Very few people are," grunted a second. "You're right there," snorted a third. Their conversation rarely rose above the intellectual level of a market ordinary; but they had the power, and could afford to be a little dull at times.

VII

ON CAUSES; WITH AN EXCURSUS ON LUCK.

I HAVE just been lunching with a man. He is either a Socialist or a Vegetarian—I forget which. On second thoughts, he cannot have been a Vegetarian, because he ate cutlets. He may have been a Philatelist; but I doubt it, and I do not fancy that it really matters. He was something—one of those things that make a man want to lead a higher life, and collar most of the conversation. He told me a good deal about it, and I know that at the time I thought it was a fine thing and an interesting thing; and I wondered why more of us did not do it; and yet I've forgotten what it was. The main point, however, is not what he was, but the fact that he was something. He had a Cause, an Enthusiasm; something that lifted him above the common ruck, something he could brag about, something that made it necessary for him to fill up papers, and sign declarations, and feel as if the nation had purchased him at his own price.

The jilted are bitter on the subject of women; the fox was malicious about the grapes that he could not reach; Tantalus was often heard to remark that undiluted water was not worth drinking. If a man sneer at Causes, it is because he himself has not any Cause; and the sneer

is idle, because he might have many Causes if he liked.
A man may be so poor that he has no effects; but he may
still have a Cause. Some of them require a subscription
of one shilling; but with more it suffices that a man shall
bother half a crown out of his friend. So, as the sneer is
not required for the consolation of the sneerer, it must
therefore be quite pointless and unprejudiced.

Personally, I must own that I have no Cause at present.
I loaf. I am utterly selfish. But I am going to select
one soon, because I feel sure that it will elevate me.
Besides, I do not see why I should be bored to death by
those of my friends who happen to be cracked—quite
cracked—about some glorious ideal, and never be able
to return their unkindness. Reciprocity is the rule of
life. You brag to me about your picture gallery for the
starving poor, and I feel at once that I must lie to you
about thought-transference. It is partly because I am just
about to ruin a Cause by my support that I feel so angry
with those selfish, flippant, trivial people who sneer at
Causes. The worst point in the sneer is its impartiality.
We do not want cold, hard, uncoloured criticism with its
shameful want of bias. We want warm, tender, muddle-
headed enthusiasm, that does not quibble about merit or
demerit, that tinges the mere critical faculty with good
feeling or bad feeling as the case may be, that is full of
humanity which is pigheadedness. But no amount of
sneers will prevent me from selecting a Cause to which I
may devote my life. The only thing which is likely to
prevent me is the difficulty of selection. There are so
many Causes, and they are all so good. Shall I be a
Philanthropist? Help the poor, and you help yourself. The

Philanthropist is the mainstay of the nation. Or shall I be
a Dipsomaniac? Help yourself, and pass the bottle. The
Dipsomaniac is the mainstay of the Budget. It would be
difficult to choose even between these two. The Dipsomaniac sacrifices more than the Philanthropist, and he is
less self-conscious; but, on the other hand, the Philanthropist is more popular and less truthful. If it be a
fine thing to help the poor, is it not an equally fine thing
to help the dear Budget? Perhaps the main distinction
between the two is that the Dipsomaniac accounts for
most of the rum, and the Philanthropist is mostly rum
in his accounts. But who can possibly decide the difference
in their merits? And these are but two : there are
thousands of others.

There once was a cuckoo-clock bird ; and after the
manner of cuckoos it did not lay wind-eggs in its own
nest. It deposited them in a mare's nest, and a stuffed
phœnix hatched them dead on the Greek Kalends of
April. It was thought at the time that the mechanical,
the impossible, and the futile had never been so beautifully
combined. Yet I have seen a man repeat the lessons that
the last pamphlet had wound him up to say, deposit a
handsome donation of his father's money in the society
that published it, crow to all his friends and expect to
see the world regenerated. The combination was quite
as beautiful, and yet people sneer at Causes ! What
great general ever lived who had not this, or a similar
faculty for combination? And though the things combined may be utterly bad in themselves, we should never
forget how very much of them we get for our money—or
our father's money, as the case may be.

But it is of little use to speak. There are few men in the world who have a Cause. We are not serious enough. We give our minds to all manner of trifles. With the exception of yourself, perhaps, I believe that I am the only man left who really wants a Cause and is unable to find one. With the rest it is sheer selfishness.

See me hit that fly on my boat's nose. Flop. Missed it. All right, you wait till it comes back again.

It seems to have aggravated that fly. It has left the boat's nose and gone for mine. I wonder if it knows that I do not like to hit my own nose hard: instinct is a marvellous thing in insects. Or it may simply be luck: luck is quite as marvellous.

I knew a man once who wanted to do serious good until luck spoilt him. He was fond of whist, and he played a good—University-good—rubber; but he felt that it was not profiting the world, and that he should like to feel that he was working for humanity when he was playing for sixpenny points.

And, firstly, it struck him that it would be a good thing to put a small tax on trumps, and help the dear Budget. He wrote to his uncle about it, because his uncle was in the House, and had once picked an earwig off Mr. Gladstone's coat, and had a good deal of influence. His uncle wrote back to say that it was a good idea, and that he had given it his earnest consideration; but that it was impracticable, because the tax would be too difficult to collect.

And, at the same time, his aunt sent him a collecting-box for the Servants' Home in Tasmania, and asked him to place it in a prominent position in his rooms and do his best for it.

So it occurred to him that here was a chance for him to impose a voluntary tax upon himself, and make his whist do some serious good. He made a vow, and repeated it aloud in these words :—" I vow that the next time I have five trumps I will put half a crown in the collecting-box for the Servants' Home in Tasmania." He told me afterwards that if the experiment had turned out well he had intended to repeat it, and do a good deal in one way or another for the Tasmanian servants. He also called my attention to the wording of the vow, which he said was important. That very night he sat down to a rubber, and started by dealing himself five trumps. They were the five lowest trumps; but my friend was surprised and pleased at the coincidence, stole softly from his place, dropped half a crown into the collecting-box on the mantelpiece, and returned without saying anything.

As it happened, one of his opponents had the remaining eight trumps, and not one of my friend's five made a trick. Ultimately he lost two trebles and the rub. It was then that he recalled the exact wording of his vow. Of course it is not an easy thing to break the bottom out of a collecting-box for the Servants' Home in Tasmania with a common brass poker; but it had to be done, and he did it.

He lost his money by gambling, which shows how wrong and foolish gambling is, and the other man won it, which proves—— What beautiful weather it was on Bank Holiday, wasn't it?

Still, it was a curious piece of luck.

A man once took out his purse in Fleet Street to buy a newspaper, and out rolled a golden sovereign. He did not see that he had dropped it. He only discovered his loss that night, and then he remembered the exact spot where he had taken out his purse. Next day he was ill in bed ; but on the day after he said he should walk back to Fleet Street and look for that sovereign. His friends laughed at him. They pointed out that in so crowded a thoroughfare the coin must have been snapped up in a moment. But the man was obstinate, and went back. He did not find the whole coin, but he found twelve shillings and sixpence of it, and an I.O.U. for the remainder.

Yes, that story's a lie. Stories about luck generally are.

That wretched, silly little fly has just perched itself on my boat's nose again. Well, I shall hit it next time—the third time.

Have you ever noticed how luck is connected with the number three—one of the religious numbers? The dream which comes true is always dreamed three times. At the cocoanuts, too, you can have three shies for a penny. There's a mystery about these things.

There once was an adopted father, and the son who had adopted him died without leaving a will, and the poor father was sonless and penniless. He felt sure that his adoptive son would never have been thoughtless enough to omit so important an arrangement as the making of a will. However, no will was found, and the property of the rich son was put up to auction. The poor father watched the sale with a gloomy face. There was the Broadwood grand-piano, on which his son had taught him his scales : he saw it disposed of to a stranger, and turned away to weep. Then a copper coal-scuttle was put up to

W. L.—VI.

4

auction, and the poor father fancied he heard a voice within him saying, "Buy the coal-scuttle! Buy the coal-scuttle!"

He had but a few pounds left, and it was a Louis XIV. coal-scuttle; but he bid for it, and ultimately secured it. With trembling hands he bore it off to the little cottage, which now was all that he had to call a home. Eagerly he opened the lid, and saw inside some small coal and a pair of broken braces.

That shows luck just as much as the other stories; but luck is like the moon—we see only one side of it. At any rate, it is quite as true as the other two stories.

That fly again! This is the third time. I feel that it is fated. I raise my paddle on high, and bring it down with one mighty whack and a murmured "Bismillah!"

I have missed the fly, and split the paddle, and could do with *something shorter* than "Bismillah!"

Now I'm going home.

VIII

IF I have gone some distance to seek solitude, it is not because I am sulky. But I never feel quite certain at this time of the year that there may not be penny steamers plying between Silver Street Bridge and Chesterton, or a Lockhart's tea and cocoa palace erected in King's. And I should hardly like to see it. Of course I did not find absolute solitude even here. The other day an apple fell on my head while I was like a child picking up pebbles on the shores of the ocean of life. I saw that there was no help for it; so I just followed precedent and discovered a natural law—that I never get anything I want. I am quite contented, consequently, that I did not find any solitude at first, and am pleasantly surprised that a large picnic party, who came and sniffed all round me suspiciously, as if they wondered why I was not muzzled, have finally decided to defile some other part of the river scenery with their happy laughter and packets of lukewarm comestibles.

I like a crowd immensely. Ditton Corner is good for the soul. So is the Strand at noon or midnight. But every one who really likes a crowd, really likes solitude.

It is pleasant enough to lie here in the hot sun, to have

a pipe that does its work properly, and to wonder what the time is, but not to be enough distressed about it to take the trouble to consult one's watch. I am finishing the "Entertainments" of Kapnides now, and I am not quite clear about the last story but one in his book. I give it, in case you have not read it.

*   *   *   *   *

It was a most beautiful cloud. Two highly respectable Athenians looked at it for a long time, and they understood beauty in Athens.

"Now, if any one were to paint that," said the first, "every one would say that it was not natural." He felt there was depth in the remark.

"I am not so sure of that," said the second, intending to be thought judicious but not disagreeable.

If the cloud had been painted, its chiefest beauty would have been omitted. For in the centre of the cloud sat the unborn soul of a girl-child. To all mortals it had no visible appearance. But the stars, as they crept slowly up for a night's work, saw with smiling eyes a graceful figure seated in the vapour, leaning a little backward, white against the crimson pillows of mist, with slender hands clasped behind a shapely head, and long dark hair and closed eyes. For it lived, but did not think, after the manner of unborn souls, which have ways distinctly of their own.

And as the sun poised over the cool, lighted sea that sang to welcome it, a noise of little tinkling silver bells was heard all down the sky; and there was some hurry and confusion amid Powers which were usually calm with the unjust, irritating, excessive calmness of a natural law.

When it was all over, no one exactly knew whose fault it was. But the Manager was summoned before the great Zeus, and reprimanded severely. "It's carelessness," said Zeus, "and that's what I can't stand. You ought to have been ready, and there are no two ways about it. You sit there in the office, wondering how long it will be before you can sneak out to your beastly lunch, and you forget that you're paid to be managing my business for me all that time."

Whether it was the Manager's fault or not, the fact remained. Down in the world, in the beautiful country just outside Athens, a boy-child had been born, and he had been born with the soul of a girl-child inside him.

"Such a piece of bungling!" grumbled Zeus, and went off to play at making orphans.

To play this game you have to be a god, and possess thunderbolts; every time you kill a father or mother you score one; if you miss, it counts nothing; if you kill anything else by mistake, you lose one.

Before the boy was grown Zeus had forgotten all about it. Perhaps this was as well for the boy, for Zeus had intended only to give him five years' life; and perhaps it was not as well.

At the age of twelve he was tall and straight. But his face was too delicate, and his eyes were the eyes that had slumbered a dreamless slumber under the closed lids of the unborn soul of a girl. And about his ways there was some sweet shyness and tenderness, or softness—names do not matter—although in courage and spirit and endurance he had no equal among his comrades. And with all his comrades he was gentle, and they loved him; but he, having no care for them nor for the parents who bore him, and angry with himself because he could feel no such care, went long, wandering walks alone, and heard strange stories told him by flowers and birds and winds.

And the years passed, and there was no change until the boy was sixteen, and then no one knew why he was so unhappy and quiet ; he himself hardly knew. But now his wanderings would take him away for days at a time. A spirit of longing possessed him, for which he had no name, and the fulfilment of it was as a dim, dancing light before him, baffling and dazzling him, and leaving him no peace. And of this neither winds, nor birds, nor flowers told him anything. And the longing drove him to climb where no others had dared to climb, or to swim far out into the cool waters of the bay, that he might come back tired and sleep through the warm fragrant night in the long grass. And ever in sleep there came one dream and told him all ; and ever when he awoke, the dream was gone from his memory. So he never knew, but always knew that he had known.

Comely maidens, with an intimate knowledge of their own best points, met him sometimes in his wanderings. And for them he cared nothing at all, and wondered why one or two of their number looked shyly at him as he passed them. They said nothing, for maidens are secretive animals ; but one with shapely arms took to herself a new bracelet ; and one with pretty pearly teeth got up a new sigh which just parted the lips without being ungraceful, and sounded extremely interesting. However, they might have painted themselves blue, and have had no effect whatever on the sorrowful youth. But they were not thus minded; and, seeing that this sad youth neither loved nor hated them, they looked out for those who understood love and hatred, and were married.

The boy's father thought it necessary to consult a physician about this strange melancholy. Besides, the youth was growing paler every day, and was listless, and cared for nothing but to lie asleep, or almost asleep, with the feathery grass rustling in a gentle whisper over him.

So the physician came, and asked several impertinent questions. Then he delivered himself upon this wise:

"It is well known that much exercise and weariness consume the spirits and substance, refrigerate the body; and such humours which nature would have otherwise concocted and expelled, it stirs up and makes them rage; which, being so enraged, diversely affect and trouble the body and mind."

"Those are comforting words," said the boy's father, who couldn't understand them.

"Keep it vague," murmured the boy softly.

"It is to the immoderate use of gymnastics," said the physician, "that I ascribe your son's melancholy. Wherefore, let him drink of a syrup of black hellebore, confected with the boiled seeds of anise, endive, mallow, fermitory, diacatholicon, hierologodium——"

"Half-time——change ends," said the boy under his breath.

"Cassia and sweet almonds," continued the physician. "And in the meantime he may drink of a broth of an exenterated chicken."

He had heard the youth's last remark. "And," he added severely, "let him beware of intempestive laughter."

So the physician went away.

" What did he say ? " asked the mother of the youth.

" Well," said the father, " he said that the boy had been growing too fast, at least he implied that, and he prescribed hierolo—— French for chicken broth, you know."

But while the doctor's prescription was being prepared, the boy went off to the cliffs; and he stretched himself at full length on the thyme, and went to sleep, and dreamed the old sweet dream, and the sun drew near to its setting, and in his pleasant sleep the boy died.

Never had there been a happier and more desirable death.

And under the burning sun a cloud was stretched like a cloth of gold.

And the two highly respectable Athenians came out to look at it.   " If I were to paint that exactly as it is," said the first, " every one would say that my picture was intensely unnatural."

" Great Zeus ! " ejaculated the second, for the first had made the remark nearly every night for rather more than sixteen years, and still thought there was a certain insight about it.

In tne golden heart of the cloud were together the soul of a youth and the soul of a young girl, two souls that had done their work and were resting.   He sat in careless happiness looking down at her: for she was stretched at his feet, making a daisy-chain with the souls of the daisies that were to bloom next year.   And ever she would look up from her work into his eyes ; and the eyes of the two were strangely alike, and soft and bright.

Into the cloud came the Manager.   He was in a terrible

hurry; for there had been great doings in Sicily, and an army had been cut to pieces, and consequently there was a press of business.

"I've called to take your numbers," he said.

They both gave the same number.

He seemed a little startled, then recovered himself, and jotted it down in his note-book. "I remember now," he said, half apologetically. "It was not entirely my fault. I had slipped out to get a glass of beer, and I told the boy to send for me if anything happened. But he thought he could manage it himself, and he blundered, and I was blamed. So you both were born in the same body. I hope you were not crowded. Zeus had intended you to be born in different bodies, and fall in love with one another down below. But you can do it up here, you know. It's not the same thing, but some people think it's better: it's much more spiritual. You will have this cloud all to yourselves for as long as you like. At any rate it was not so hard on you as it was on the girl's body, which had to be born without any soul at all—but I am told that she made money out of it. Well, I must be off; good evening."

So the Manager departed, and they were alone, and they floated away into the night when the night came. And the sea sang beneath them, and the wind was warm and perfumed with flowers.

"I love you for ever and ever," he said.

The same remark had just occurred to her—not strikingly original, perhaps, but both were satisfied with it.

IX

ON ASSOCIATIONS: TOGETHER WITH A LAST ANECDOTE
FROM THE "ENTERTAINMENTS" OF KAPNIDES.

I THINK *Zeitgeist* has grown lazy; I had meant to take
it a long way to-day, but it simply stopped at the first
shady spot it could find, and stretched itself there. One
has to smoke a little brown tobacco to keep off the midges,
but otherwise I do not mind much. I would not make
use of my superior strength to force a tired boat to do more
than it wanted to do. Besides, *Zeitgeist* has earned some
consideration. It has behaved excellently; in fact, it has
almost been morbid in the politeness with which it has
avoided running into other boats lately. Somebody, I see,
has put a bottle of cider into the canoe. How thoughtless
of him! There are a corkscrew and a drinking-horn as
well. Perhaps it's all for the best.

The taste of cider should be full of associations. It
should recall orchards in Devonshire; and rustic inns with
porches, and honeysuckle, and earwigs; and the simple
village maiden who got to be rather fond of the stranger
artist, and cried a little in her simple village way when he
went back again to civilisation. I am starving for dreamy
poetry and pleasant memories this morning; I wish this
cider had such beautiful associations for me. But it has

not. To me cider is cider, and it is nothing more. I have never been in a Devonshire orchard; and I am not an artist; I have never drawn anything.

Except corks. By the way, I may as well put that bottle of cider in the shallow water here. It will cool it. Then, afterwards, I may be able to forgive the person who put it into my canoe.

I am not sure that people do not set too much store by associations. There is an old tune that most people have forgotten, I dare say; perhaps it is not very good music; in fact, I would take an affidavit that it is the nastiest, tuniest tune I ever heard, and yet it has associations for me. It recalls to me my landlady's daughter; it was the tune she loved most and played most frequently; she was rather an ugly girl, too. But I do not value the tune any more on that account; I believe it makes me hate it more bitterly.

I should think that cider must be almost cool by now, but I will give it another minute or two.

I suppose it is for the sake of associations that people have their dead pets stuffed, or have portions of them made into tobacco-pouches or paper-knives. I never had any pet myself except one solitary, evil dog; he was an original dog, and was perfectly good-tempered with everybody except his master. I am thankful to say that I possess absolutely nothing which reminds me of him. The smell of tar has curious associations for me. It reminds me of a day when I drove frantically in the direction of Liverpool Street, with the intention of catching the 10.30. I had offered my cabby vast sums to get me there in time, and he certainly did his best. I did not stop to take a ticket, but dashed across the platform, and entered the train just as it was moving out. I sank back on the cushions with a sigh of relief. One gets so much pleasure out of *just* doing a thing. Then I found out that the train which I had entered was not the 10.30, was not going to the same place, and was not thinking of stopping anywhere for some considerable time. Perhaps you wonder why the smell of tar should remind me of this. So do I. I have not the least notion why it is.

One must not expect to see the reason for the connection always. Why are the girls with the biggest feet always devoted to quite inferior works of fiction? Why are clean-shaven men always cynical?

Then of course there are the tender, romantic associations. A good deal might be said about them. In the meantime I can't think where I've put that corkscrew. Ah! here it is, sitting under one of the cushions and laughing at me. Now for the cider, with a golden glow in it like the curls of the love-god himself.

And flat—miserably flat.

＊　　＊　　＊　　＊　　＊

As I said, *Zeitgeist* does not care to move about much. So I have amused myself with reading the last anecdote in the "Entertainments" of Kapnides. Here it is :—

A general feeling of content prevailed in the house of Zeus & Co. "We shall declare," said Zeus, "such a dividend as never was."

"We shall," said Co.

Zeus & Co. occupied the two thrones at the back of the large hall. During the last spring-cleaning, Zeus had ordered his own throne to be regilded. Nothing had been done to the other throne, which was occupied by Co. But Co. was quite humble. As a general rule he merely echoed the sentiments of Zeus. If he felt the difference between the two thrones, he had never mentioned it. Perhaps it might be as well to notice that all the shares were in the hands of Zeus & Co. They were the directors, and also the shareholders. By this arrangement much unpleasantness was avoided.

But at this moment an old gentleman in a very shiny coat rose from the desk at the farther end of the hall, and stepped towards the thrones. He looked at Zeus, coughed a little nervously, and began :

" Mr. Zeus, and also Mr. Co., you will excuse me, but I've a little matter to bring before you, in my position as Chief Agent in the Punishment Department."

" By all means," said Zeus kindly. " There's nothing wrong, I hope. It's a good department."

" A very good and profitable department," echoed Co.

" Well, Mr. Zeus, you will probably remember that you assigned to me a young subordinate, a mere boy, called Eros."

" I remember," said Zeus. " He was not to draw any regular salary."

" Precisely so," replied the Agent. " He just took his small commission on every broken heart. Well, up to the present I've had no complaint to make of him. He did his work well and cheerfully. The Suicide Section used to send me in most favourable reports of him. I had even intended to recommend him for promotion."

" But without increase of salary, I hope," said Zeus. " The shareholders would never stand that, you know."

"They simply wouldn't tolerate it for a minute," echoed Co. It was not supposed to be generally known that Zeus & Co. were the only shareholders.

"No, sir," answered the Agent. "I should have left the question of salary to you. I hope I know my place, sir. But, if you will believe it, that boy actually wants to resign the post he holds already. He got mixed up in that Psyche business a good deal, you know. I never knew the rights of the case exactly; but I do know that he's not been the same boy since, and takes no pleasure in his work at all."

"Well, show him in," said Zeus irritably, "and I'll have a word or two to say to him."

"I wonder," suggested Co., "if the Agent can have been fool enough to let the boy know that he was a punishment and not a blessing?"

At this moment the Agent, who had retired, reappeared with Eros. He was a handsome boy, but it was evident that he was very angry. His eyes flashed, and tears stood in them. He made no obeisance to Zeus, but with a rapid movement unslung his bow and quiver from his shoulders, and snapt bow and arrows, one after another, across his knee, flinging them down on the floor of the hall.

"I've had enough of that," he said shortly, setting his lips tight.

"Are you aware," said Co. solemnly, "that what you have just broken is the property of the shareholders?"

"And are you aware," thundered Zeus, "what the dickens you're talking about? Explain yourself."

The boy burst into tears. "I *won't* do it any more,"

he sobbed. "I *won't.* I'm not a blessing; I'm a curse. And I'm not going to be your servant, because you hate everybody."

"No," said Co. quietly; "we love them."

"Then what does your first rule mean?" asked the boy fiercely.

"The first rule," replied Co., "is that twenty years shall not be enough to make a life, and ten minutes shall be more than enough to spoil it. We made that rule to stop people spoiling their lives."

Zeus rubbed his hands softly together, and smiled, and said nothing.

"I did not mind once," the boy went on, "when I made women weep and men rave. I do now. It's always the same thing. They long, and long, and cannot obtain; and then the weaker sort kill themselves, and the stronger sort grow cruel. Or, if they obtain, misery in one form or another follows. I resign my post."

"Just pass me that thunderbolt," said Zeus, in an unpleasant voice.

"Oh, you can kill me," the boy exclaimed, contemptuously, "I care nothing for that. I wish I had never lived."

"But you mistake," said Co., suavely, "you mistake; Mr. Zeus had no intention of killing you. You have a right to resign your post if you like. He was going to kill a young girl named Psyche."

"What for?" gasped Eros.

"Oh, for sport."

There was a moment's silence. Then Eros spoke in a hard, unnatural voice. "I will go back to my work,

Zeus, and do it better than ever, if you will not kill Psyche."

"Very well," said Zeus kindly. "I don't want to be disagreeable ; as long as I kill somebody, it doesn't matter. Now, trot along to your work, my boy, and I won't kill Psyche."

So the boy went back to his work, and did it better than ever.

"That was a good idea of yours, Co.," said Zeus, after a moment's pause.

"Very much may be done by kindness," replied Co. "Don't you think this throne of mine looks a little shabby beside yours?"

"I'll give the order to have it regilded," said Zeus affably.

But, if things go on like this, it will be "Co. & Zeus" soon.

*　　　*　　　*　　　*

It's getting late time for me to take *Zeitgeist* home again.

A curate was once complaining to me about certain hardships that he suffered at the hands of his vicar. "And, above all," he said, "I am never allowed to preach an evening sermon. I get no chances. The vicar always preaches the evening sermons." There was a good deal of justice in the complaint ; we are all naturally more righteous in the evening. When the light dies behind the stained windows, and the music speaks, and through the open doors you can smell the syringa-bushes, then—for some reason that I know not—it is more easy to think oneself a sinner and to wish one were not. Preaching would naturally be more effective at such a time.

It is evening now, and I have been thinking about the different things that I am going to eat shortly. I do not know what is wrong with me that I should be so low. But external circumstances that suggest one line of thought are always liable to suggest the exact opposite. It has been proved by statistics that two-thirds of the best English jokes are invented, but not necessarily spoken, at funerals. Perhaps this accounts for the depression one always has to conceal when one hears of the joy or success of a dear friend.

Zeitgeist will have a long rest now—until my return. I could wish for some reasons that I had a more complete control over that boat ; that, when I started out with it, I could be more definitely sure where it was going ; that, in short, its nature was less petulant. However, there is a charm in uncertainty. I forgive it everything.

THE NINE MUSES MINUS ONE

I.

CLIO'S STORY: CHARLES MARIUS.

ON a beautiful summer night of last long vacation a cloud sailed slowly out of the west. The sun was going down; the honest worker had fallen asleep over his books, and in his dream was standing before a booking office in the Bay of Tarentum and asking for a second aorist return to Clapham; the jubilant whist player, holding the situation in his hand, had exhausted the trumps, and was bringing in the rest of a long suit; the mere conversationalist had worked in that epigram again, and the mere athlete, who did not believe in that fancy kind of talk, had gone away to drink a little good beer; the fiery bedmaker had just gone round to the kitchens, to tell the men precisely what she thought about them: in fact, everything—except the cloud—was much as usual. But the cloud was extraordinary.

It was granted to me to see that cloud close at hand, to stand in its midst, to hear what was spoken there, while I remained unseen and unheard. I do not wish to speak of myself much, because it seems to me vain and immodest; but I must say that I believe the real reason why I was permitted to behold the Muses, and to hear the stories which they told to one another to while away the summer night, is that my nature is singularly pure, and good, and spiritual, and free from grossness, and beautiful. So, I feel sure, is your nature, my dear reader, although in a less degree.

In the front of the cloud hung a rosy curtain of some delicate tissue, and behind this curtain was the rose-lit room in which the Muses were grouped. Clio was standing erect. She wore a long and ample robe; her figure was stately; her look was the look of a handsome, learned woman, who is on the brink of her thirtieth year. In one hand was an open roll of paper, on which gilt letters were blazoned. She was looking down upon the towers, and steeples, and house-tops of Cambridge, and on the slow river winding like a reluctant silver corkscrew through the beautiful meadows of Grantchester.

Behind her, seven of her sisters, picturesquely grouped, reclined on a low divan at the farther end of the room. They all were beautiful in different ways. Their robes, snow-white and pearly-grey, golden and crimson and deep-sea blue, made a poem of colour.

And on the mosaic floor, kneeling on one knee, bending over a little tripod that supported a brazier, was one who wore no robe, but the long night of her beautiful hair. Mockery was on her lips, but dreams were in her eyes. She seemed a young girl of seventeen. She was Erato, who sings to us of love. The picture of her in the classical dictionaries is absurdly wrong. Beside her on the floor lay her lyre and a curious golden casket. From the brazier a thin, wandering line of fragrant smoke came up, and hovered in the room.

There was a moment's silence. Then Clio turned round to her sisters. "We will stay here," she said, "for a little while. This is Granta; and here are gathered young men who are truly gymnasts and yet follow the Muses. For they do all of them seek after culture, and love naught but the reading of many learned books, and the hearing of the wisdom of their teachers; and they all strive to lead the higher life."

Terpsichore gave a curious little cough. I have no certain idea what it meant; but it seemed to imply in some way that she had been there before. The grave and stately Clio never noticed it.

"Yes, we will stay, and tell to one another improving stories," she went on. "Cupid! Cupid!" she called.

A curtain at the side of the room was flung aside, and in came a little winged boy, with laughing eyes, naked but for the quiver that hung from the shoulders. He does a good deal for the Muses, but not in a menial way. They all smiled when he came in. He stood by the side of Erato, who evidently petted him a good deal, drawing one strand of her dark hair through his little rosy fingers—but he was looking at Clio.

"Cupid," said the grave Muse, "we would stay here: let the wind blow our cloud no farther." He nodded his head, turned to go, and then lingered, still playing with Erato's hair.

"Erato," he whispered in her ear, "my bow-string is frayed. Let me make a bow-string of your hair."

"No—perhaps—not now. You wicked little boy!" she said, looking up in his face and laughing.

"Then soon," he whispered again, and passed once more behind the curtain. I do not know what he did, but the wind ceased, and the cloud remained still. Clio took her place on the divan. "Who shall begin?" she asked.

"Oh, you!" they all cried together.

"You're the eldest, you know," added Erato, a little maliciously. Erato had taken a cushion from the divan, and stretched herself very lazily on the floor. I am afraid the other Muses were all anxious to get Clio's story over as soon as possible. History was her province, and she was so exceedingly historical as to be sometimes almost dull.

"Very well, then. I will begin," said Clio. "The number of temporal lords summoned by writ to the parliaments of the House of Plantagenet was exceedingly various."

Clio paused. There was a sly, mischievous look on Erato's face; she stretched out one hand to the golden casket, and took from it a little powder, which she dropped into the brazier. A strange, pungent odour came up from it. I do not know what it was, but it had a curious effect.

"I think I will begin again," said Clio. "That's the wrong story."

Then she told the story which follows. I am afraid the powder had a little to do with it.

* * * * *

With the battle of Waterloo the last hope of Charles was humbled in the dust. Three years afterwards he was found by the lictors seated in a poor third-class compartment in the railway junction which was erected

on the site of that scene of carnage, and still retains
the name of Waterloo. Charles surveyed them from the
window, calmly and unflinchingly. " Go," he said, " and
tell the Carthaginians that you have seen Marius seated
in the South-Eastern Express for Charing Cross."

His request was never carried out. It was almost
impossible to book through to Carthage, and it was too
far to walk. With tears in their eyes, the lictors
walked sorrowfully away to the refreshment-room. The
train steamed out of the station and arrived a week later
at Charing Cross, a little tired, but in fairly good condition.
Charles Marius levied two benevolences on the arrival
platform, and conferred a monopoly on the bookstall ;
but he was not looking at all well. The marshes of
Minturnæ, and a rooted dislike to being called a man of
blood, had preyed on his mind, and made him appear
haggard and anxious. He was met under the clock by
the aged Menenius Agrippa, Socrates, John Bradshaw,
the Spanish Ambassador, and others. John Bradshaw was
naturally the first to speak.

" As Serjeant-at-Law and President of the High Court of
Justice, it is my painful duty to——"

" Stay," interrupted Menenius Agrippa. " I once told a
fable to the Plebeians, and it did good. It is not generally
known, and it may be of service in the present critical
juncture. Charles Marius, you man of blood, listen. Once
upon a time the members refused to work any longer for the
Belly, which led a lazy life, and grew fat upon——"

" Don't, my dear friend, don't," said the Spanish Ambassador piteously. " We know it by heart. It's all in
little Smith."

"But it may do good," said the aged Menenius. "How far had I got? Oh yes—and grew fat upon their toils. But receiving no longer any nourishment from the Belly, they soon began to——"

At this moment a cheerful porter, with a merry cry of "Now then, stoopid!" ran a heavy truckful of luggage into the aged Menenius and bowled him over. This gave John Bradshaw an opportunity to resume his remarks:

"It seemeth to me that the time hath now gone by when the telling of fables might serve the body politick; and seeing what grave charges have been exhibited against you, Charles Marius, you man of blood, and duly proven before me, it behoveth us rather to inquire into the method which shall be deemed most suitable for your execution."

He went on to point out that there were many methods of execution, but that it was most agreeable to the sense of the nation that Charles Marius should be taken to a very small, very cheap, very dirty, very Italian restaurant; and that he should drink there one bottle of that sound dinner-wine Raisonola at eleven shillings the dozen.

"We hereby give our royal word," said Charles Marius; but he was sternly checked by the Serjeant-at-Law.

"We need nothing of your royal word, having in former times had too much of it. I myself will walk first, accompanied by the Spanish Ambassador and Menenius Agrippa. You, Socrates, will accompany that man of blood, Charles Marius, and administer to him the consolations of your philosophy. You others will remain."

The sad procession filed out of Charing Cross Station. Menenius Agrippa looked a little angry, and was brushing the dust from his toga; but the Spanish Ambassador and

John Bradshaw were intensely stately and dignified. Behind them walked Socrates and Charles Marius. Socrates began at once:

"Seeing, my friend, that you are about to be executed, let us speak of execution. For it is well to speak always of the thing which is the present thing. So, setting aside your misconduct under H. Metellus Stanleius in Africa, let us discuss this execution. Now, I have often wondered why to the many it always seems an evil to be executed. For if a will be duly executed, it takes force therefrom. Now, to acquire force is plainly to be reckoned among the good things. Therefore to be executed must be good and desirable. Or shall we say rather that words have no meaning?"

"Go to the deuce!" said Charles Marius sulkily. "We offered John Bradshaw our royal word, and he refused to take it. So we won't talk at all."

And he never said another word until they were all five seated at one table in the Italian restaurant. A melancholy waiter of no nationality brought a soiled bill of fare; he also added two forks and a mustard-pot as a kind of after-thought.

"Bring," said John Bradshaw, "one bottle of Raisonola and one glass."

"Ver' well," said the waiter sadly, flicking a dead fly off the table with one end of his napkin. "It will be a shilling, if you please."

"Pay afterwards," said John Bradshaw sharply.

The waiter shrugged his shoulders. "I am ver' sorry, but we mos' always ask for ze monny before we bring ze Raisonola. We haf our orders. You see we haf often had a trouble to get ze monny afterwards from ze heirs. Tree weeks ago two gemmens kom in and order ze Raisonola. They trink it, and die all over ze floor." (An expressive shrug of shoulders came in again here.) "We sweep 'em up, and throw 'em away, and they pay us nossin—nossin at all. It is all so moch loss." His hands were turned outward, deprecatingly.

"Look here, my man," said Menenius Agrippa quickly. "Once upon a time the members refused to work any longer for the Belly, which——"

"Dry up," thundered John Bradshaw. "We must pay,' he added. "And it so befalleth that I have not my purse, but the Spanish Ambassador——"

The Ambassador explained that he had only Spanish coins with him, which would not be accepted. Socrates hastily added the information that he always took his money straight home to Xantippe, and that if he was short that night there would be unpleasantness.

Menenius said that he had no money, but would be glad to continue his fable. "Let's see. Where was I? Oh, I know—any longer for the Belly, which——"

"Do drop it," sighed the Spanish Ambassador pathetically.

"Silence," said John Bradshaw. "Charles, be a man, and pay for your own execution."

Charles offered his note of hand and his royal word.

> He nothing common did or mean
> Upon that memorable scene.

But the waiter refused them. And the five were compelled to leave the restaurant. There was a crowd round the

door. When they had got clear of the crowd, one of
their number was missing. It was Charles Marius.

The rest of the story is well known. Charles Marius
escaped to St. Helena, and spent the rest of his life in
collaborating with Dr. Gauden on a novel called "Eikon
Basilike." The failure of the execution preyed upon John
Bradshaw's mind, and in a fit of madness he wrote the
time-tables which bear his name. Menenius Agrippa became a diner-out, and acquired the surname of "History,"
because he always repeated himself. The Ambassador
still lives in his castle in Spain.

      *   *   *   *   *

Clio had finished. "Thank you so much," said the
other Muses.

II

EUTERPE'S STORY: THE GIRL AND THE MINSTREL.

THERE was silence for a few moments. Erato, stretched lazily on the floor, looking up at the dim-lit roof of the cloud-chamber, let her pretty lips curve half-way to a smile, when she checked herself suddenly; she never could keep her thoughts still for a moment,— they flew from poor Clio's story to a story of her own. She was thinking now of a hot summer night in Sicily, and of one who walked across the low hills, with flocks pattering softly after him, and seen but indistinctly in those fragrant moments when the evening touches the darkness. She thought of him. As he went, he piped a melody—a simple strain enough, but with one of those quaint refrains that nestle down in the memory of a man. Ah—and afterwards !

"Clio," she said, drawing a long breath, "I have a story, sweet and fit for a summer night, a story of the joyousness, and rapture, and sorrow of Love. Will you hear it ? "

"Ah, yes, Clio !" said Terpsichore. "Erato once told me a story, and it was so lovely and dreamy. It had the temper of soft valse music. One's heart throbbed to it : one lived to it, as it were. Let us hear Erato's story."

"Not just yet, I think," answered Clio. "We must

not forget that Granta lies beneath us. Far down below
our feet, one sits—a young man with red hair—amid
many dictionaries. He is turning into Latin elegiacs
those beautiful lines—I quote from memory—

> His head was bare, his matted hair
> Was shaved to keep him cool.

Already he has seven feet in his hexameter, and knows it
not, because the gods do not like him. If we let thoughts
of love stray forth from our cloud-chamber, and flutter down
into that young man's red head, I fear that he would never
get the pentameter at all. No, Erato, to these young men
love is a disturbing influence; they avoid the maidens, and
care only for a surer knowledge of Greek accentuation.
When they have all gone to bed, you shall tell your story;
great personages in history have fallen in love; I myself
have no prejudice against it. But you may choose which
of us shall tell the next story."

Erato sighed, and glanced round the room. When her
eyes fell on Euterpe her face brightened. And truly Euterpe
was good to see : she had a wonderful grace of body, and
fresh gladness in her eyes; yet there was a depth in the
look of her; it was the look of one not easily understood,
of one who could feel a sorrow.

"I choose Euterpe, because she is so beautiful."

A little flush came into Euterpe's cheeks; her lips
parted, showing her small white teeth. She was ever
shy and quiet.

"I would sooner sing to you," she said. "I am more
used to singing."

"No, dear, it must be a story," said Clio firmly.

"And perhaps a song will come into it," added Erato sweetly.

Then Euterpe told this story. And all the time that she was telling it Erato sat gazing upward into Euterpe's eyes.

        *   *   *   *   *

The child came through the forest. The big trees grew close together, and creeping plants hung like heavy serpents from their boughs. The sun found its way through, here and there, among the broad, smooth leaves, and made splashes of light on the red gold of the child's hair. One bird called to another; every now and then there was a flutter among the leaves, or the quick rustle of some small live thing in the tall grasses and brushwood below, and a scented wind kept singing of a land of rest where the good winds go when they die. From far away one could hear the low roar of a lion, as he stood by the margin of the distant morass, looking over stretches of sand and spaces of still water to the line of grey hills that seemed to be the end of the world.

The child was very fair. Her hair was glorious; her eyes were blue; her young limbs were white, and strong, and graceful. Yet one might see a fierce look in the blue eyes, and splashes of crimson here and there on the white limbs, and her breath came quickly; for it was in her nature to torture and to kill, and she knew no better thing. In one hand she dragged along the body of a young wild cat, scarcely more than a kitten. She lived ever in the open air, and she was fleet and fearless. All the morning she had chased it, until it was weary; yet, although it was young, it had fought long and fiercely. On the hand that

dragged it along were the marks of its claws and teeth;
thick drops of blood fell slowly on to its body, and its fur
was wet and stained. The child wore a living, tortured,
fluttering necklace. She had caught the butterflies one by
one, choosing those which were brightest in colour, and had
threaded a spiked tendril through the soft bodies to make
herself the necklace. She liked the tickling fuss and flutter
that the butterflies made against her smooth skin, as they
hung there and died slowly.

A great purple flower, that grew low down on the ground,
lifted its brightness towards her as she passed : " And, oh ! "
sighed the flower, " she is fair, and sweet would it be if
she would take me and wear me gently at her breast." The
child did not know the voice of flowers ; but she stooped
down and tore off the purple petals one by one. From the
cup of the flower rolled a big golden bee : he had been
sleeping there. For one second he buzzed on the ground,
trying to remember where he was and to understand what
had happened. In that second the child had swiftly seized
a stone, and so she crushed most of the bee, leaving it
enough life to let it feel the agony of death. She flung
down the body of the wild cat, and ran on for a few steps,
with a laugh on her red mouth. Then she stopped again
where a nest was built in a bush with very dark leaves and
little white globes of flowers. In the nest were three young
birds : two of these she cast to the ground and killed at
once : she held the third in her small hot hands for a
second, and a kind of frenzy came on her, and she made
her firm teeth meet in its neck. For a little while she
stood shuddering, and then she passed onwards, but more
slowly. Slowly she came through the forest in her fairness

and cruelty, caring nothing for her own beauty, and knowing nothing better than her cruelty.

And it chanced that she came to the place where the minstrel sat in pleasant shade on a mossy curve of a tree's root. In his hands was his lyre, and music came from it like falling water. The child crept into the brushwood, and hid herself, and listened. And the minstrel sang :

> Far away is the land where all things go,
> The rest of the winds that have ceased to blow,
> The peace of the rose whose leaves lie low,
> Scattered and dead, where roses grow.
> > Far away ! far away !
>
> There the dead bird takes a song again,
> And the steed has rest from the spur and rein,
> And the dead man learns that all were vain—
> All the old struggles, and joys, and pain.
> > Far away ! far away !
>
> And the light on their eyes is a wondrous light,
> Where there is not day and there is not night,
> Where the fallen star once more grows bright
> That fell into darkness out of the height—
> > Far away ! far away !
>
> Let me win there ere the break of day,
> Ere the first faint light o'er the hills grows grey,
> I am tired of my work and tired of my play,
> And I'll make better songs in the land far away,—
> > Far away ! far away !

The voice ceased ; but the music of the lyre still flowed on, and the minstrel looked upwards towards the sky. No word of cruelty had been in the song ; but through the music her first knowledge of gentleness came to the child, and she saw that she had been cruel. She crouched there amid the tall rank grasses; her face had grown whiter and whiter; her eyes were strained and piteous, but there was no tear in them. With trembling fingers she unfastened the living fluttering necklace, and gently killed all the butterflies to spare them torture. Then she flung herself prone on the ground, with her forehead on her linked hands; her red lips quivered a little, but the relief of tears came not. "Ah!" she moaned, "why was I so cruel? Why did I never know?" The wind played with her hair, moving it caressingly.

As the child lay there, and the minstrel played on and on, the sky above grew darker. There was no need now for pleasant shade. Over the line of grey hills that seemed to be the end of the world rested the storm-clouds, black and purple. Suddenly the air became quite still, as if it were waiting for something. Was it the roar of the lion or the voice of the storm that sounded dimly afar off?

Once more the minstrel raised his voice to song, and anger was in his eyes:

> The pure white flower grew up in the way
> Where the wild cat's whelp went forth to play.
>
> And the whelp rent the flower for the gold within,
> And a child slew the whelp for its soft warm skin.
>
> And the lion slew the child for a draught of blood,
> And the river swept the lion away in its flood.
>
> And the gods dried the river in its deep stone bed,
> And all from the flower to the stream were dead.
>
> We are things that the gods make sport upon:
> We shall have no peace till the gods are gone.

The child had raised herself to watch the minstrel. As

he sang the last words the skies seemed to snap overhead ; a quick flash shot downwards, like the thrust of ghostly steel. For a moment the child's eyes were dazzled ; then the loud roar of thunder seemed to fill the forest and the sky. When she looked again she saw that the minstrel had fallen forward on his face ; by his side was his lyre, with the strings broken and smouldering ; from his body, charred by the lightning, delicate strays of smoke curled up. The child came, and knelt by the side of the dead minstrel. She raised his head, and looked piteously upon it, for the beauty had all gone out of it now ; then she pressed her little red lips to the blackened lips of the dead man, and went on her way. It was the first kiss she had ever given.

And still she did not weep ; but the blood in her veins seemed to be as fire, and strange voices were sounding in her head. When the evening fell she stood by the edge of the swamp. Out of a dim cavern crept an old lion, and looked at her with green, hungry eyes. His lips curled a little backward. The child called to him : "Come, then ! I have been seeking for you ! Torture me, and then let me die !"

The lion turned swiftly round, and fled with a howl back into the cavern.

The child wandered on. She ate the black poison berries, but they would not hurt her. At last, when the moon was up, she saw a dark, deep pool, and flung herself into it ; but the pool cast her back again on to the shore She was fain to die, and to atone ; but the gods knew their business better than to allow it.

And still she walks through the forest, seeking rest and finding it not, and she speaks to none. Only sometimes at night, when the golden moon comes up behind the low grey hills, she sings in a sweet child's voice a few lines of a remembered song:

> Let me win there ere the break of day,
> Ere the first faint light o'er the hills grows grey !
> I am tired of my work and tired of my play,
> And I'll make better songs in the land far away,—
>   Far away ! far away !

And the gods are immensely amused.

      *   *   *   *   *

"Thanks," said Thalia, "though I don't care much for those fanciful high-toned stories."

But Erato rose, and seated herself on the divan by Euterpe's side, and wound one arm round her waist, and kissed her on the lips. I thought they looked rather pretty and poetical; but I don't go in much for that kind of thing myself.

III.

A SHORT pause, and then Erato spoke, addressing Clio:

"Clio, my dear and reverend sister, do you think these young men below us, in the colleges, have gone to bed yet?"

"My dear child," said Clio, "you could hardly expect me to—— well, as far as I can judge, some of them are still up and at work. The young red-headed man is stamping up and down his room, as if he were angry. He has discovered that his hexameter would not do, for

His head was bare, his matted hair,

and he has been trying it a different way. Now he moans: ' "Caput erat nudum "—and the "a" 's short, and I wish I was dead!'"

"I asked the question," said Erato, "because a story has just occurred to me, which I should like to tell you. I read it in the French. I don't think it would hurt the young men, even if they could hear it. I'll tone it down a little, of course. There's one splendid part where the husband——" She paused suddenly.

"Yes," said Thalia drily. "In those pretty French

stories there generally is one splendid part where the husband——" and she also paused suddenly. She looked at Erato, and they both smiled.

"Certainly not! Most certainly not!" said Clio at once. "You must remember, Erato, that this is not the Greek civilisation. The English have got beyond that: they have advanced; they sweep through the deep while the stormy winds do blow, and hearts of oak are their men, and they'd take a cup o' kindness yet on the place where the old hoss died. I make these last remarks on the authority of their own favourite songs, of which I have made a special study for my book on National Misfortunes. I assure you, Erato, that any University paper which printed your story would be ruined."

"Ah, well!" answered Erato. "I have heard it said that Love's a lost art nowadays" She paused a second, and then added: "Perhaps—perhaps they are happier without it."

"I don't think so," said Terpsichore. "Everything depends on the way you take it. Some take their love laughing, and some take it crying. I always take it laughing myself. Either way, you're happier for it."

"Really, Terpsichore," murmured Clio reprovingly.

Terpsichore did not heed her. "Where they are so wrong nowadays is in taking their love commercially; in other words, they do not *love*; they simple acquire all rights in a cheap housekeeper or an expensive table ornament. They are so much too judicious. Yet sometimes—well, there was a man—shall I go on?"

"Yes, do," said Erato.

And this is the way that Terpsichore went on :—

　　　*　　　　*　　　　*　　　　*　　　　*

There was a man once—not very long ago—who was poor,
but artistic ; and during his life he had rather more than his
share of coincidences. It happened one autumn that he
was amusing himself by wandering about a country that
was good enough for an artist, but failed to attract many
tourists because it did not boast enough places where you
had to pay for admission. He had stayed a few days in a
little village, where there was one street that went tumbling
downhill, sometimes with cottages on each side, sometimes
through clumps of stunted trees, sometimes with the open
heath all round it. It happened one night that he was
wandering down this street, and had reached one of those
places where the street turned into a country lane for a time,
or rather for a space. He was smoking, and humming to
himself a song that he had heard Viola sing a few months
before.

Viola had taken very fair hold of the town that season.
It was not only that she sang divinely ; she was beautiful,
and a little mysterious. The numerous stories told about
her were rendered probable by her beauty, which was rather
wicked ; but no one could be certain about them because
she was so mysterious. Besides, many of the stories were
self-contradictory.

On one side of the road was a cottage, standing by itself,
and partly screened by the shrubs which grew in the small
garden in front of it. Here the man stopped short, for the
lower windows of the cottage were open, and from within he
could hear some one singing the very song which he had just
been humming. Some one ? Why, it could be no other
than Viola herself who was singing it like that ! He had
always been interested in Viola, although he had seen her

only on the stage. It was her reputation that she loved splendour and luxury. What could she be doing in this quiet, out-of-the-way village ?

He leaned over the low garden gate, resting his elbows on the top of it, and listened until the song's conclusion. The room in the cottage was brightly lighted, and the curtains were not drawn over the window ; he had heard rightly ; it *was* Viola. He could see her distinctly. She was standing with her face towards the garden ; and the man watched her attentively. The mystery increased. Her dress was brilliant, not the dress that a woman would put on in solitude and in a country village. She was wearing her diamonds too—those diamonds about which every story had been told except the true one. What was the reason for it all ? Was this simply her passion for splendour, existing even when the splendour was to have no witnesses. The little, shabby, taciturn old woman who acted as her companion in London was seated at the piano, and had been playing the music for her song. But surely Viola would not have made herself so magnificent simply on her account.

It suddenly dawned on him that he was doing rather a mean thing by watching Viola in this way. He would not look any more, but he would wait, in case she should be going to sing again. That was love of music—not curiosity.

But even as he was making this decision the door of the cottage opened, and Viola came out. She walked straight up the pathway towards the gate on which the man was leaning ; there was not the least hesitation about her.

" I wonder how on earth she managed to see me in this darkness ?" he thought. " Well, I'm not going to run away. I will wait, and make my apologies to her. I expect she will be angry with me. Well, she should not leave the windows open when she sings, if she does not want people to stop and listen."

As she drew near to him she murmured a few words in Italian, as if she were pleased about something ; he conjectured that much, for he could not understand Italian. Then she astonished him by placing her hands on his shoulders, and kissing him, once, passionately.

It flashed across him for an instant that she had been expecting some one else, and had made a mistake. Now he understood the dress, the diamonds—everything.

"Excuse me, my dear lady," he said, "but you are kissing the wrong face—are you not?" He afterwards thought that he might have expressed himself better, but he was agitated.

She, on the other hand, never lost her composure for a second. She spoke in English, with the faintest possible stammer :

"Yes, th—thanks ; it *is* the wrong face. Would you t—take it away?"

He retired at once, walked twenty yards down the road, and then met the full humour of the situation. He laughed a long, suppressed laugh. He went on and on, away from the village, out over the heath, away from the haunts of men. And, as he walked, the humour of the situation vanished again ; but the night was full of her music, her queenliness, the fragrant charm of her presence. "Viola," he said softly, "Viola, what a heavenly mistake ! "

Three years passed away. The poor but artistic man grew slowly wealthy in those years. The exaltation of that night never left him ; he was full of brightness and happi-

ness ; his work was all light and strength. He grew popular—
partly by reason of his excellent spirits, and partly because
of his finer qualities.   His luck was proverbially good ; but
he had enough hope, optimism, and vigour to have carried
him safely through the most trying fortunes.   His reputation
was at its brightest when his death came.

He was in an accident—a commonplace railway accident
—an accident that passed over a dishonest commercial
traveller in one compartment, and killed the artist in the
next.   There was a short period, however, chiefly occupied by delirium, between the accident and the man's
death.

It was at the end of the delirium that he turned to the
friend who was by his bedside, and asked abruptly :

" Have I been speaking of Viola ? "

" Yes ; of course I wouldn't—— "

" Of course.   All the time ? "

" All the time."

" Were you surprised ? "

" Well, I have known you most of your life, and I never
heard you speak of her before—not in that way at all.   I
did not know that you had been her lover."

" I was not.   But once, before she left England, I was
—I was her lover's under-study.   I have lived on it ever
since," he added, after a pause.

Then, through some queer freak of the brain, the humour
of the mistaken kiss appealed to him again, and he began
to laugh—uncontrollably, as if the thing had just happened.

Laughter was the worst thing possible for him in that
state.   He died laughing.

*   *   *   *   *   *

" I suppose she—Viola—didn't care," said Erato thoughtfully, when Terpsichore had finished her story.

"You forget that she had some one else to think about. Did you ever know a woman yet that thought twice, by way of pity, about a man she did *not* love, when she had a man that she *did* love to think about ? "

"N—no," Erato replied.

There was a moment's pause. "Personally I don't mind," said Clio, "but—considering where we are—do you think that last story quite—quite judicious ? "

IV

MELPOMENE'S STORY : THE CURSED PIG.

" I 'M rather thirsty," said Erato to Clio. Erato had stretched herself once more on the mosaic floor of the cloud-room, with enough cushions to make herself comfortable. "So am I," said Terpsichore.

"Well, considering how very hot the night is, I am not surprised. Cupid !"

The little petulant boy came laughing into the room, and nodded his head in reply to the order which Clio gave him. Then he brought in a silver tray covered with fragile glasses of nectar. All the Muses drank nectar except Melpomene. She had a look of intense gloom, and she drank blood-and-seltzer from a very large tumbler with a very bad curse cut in Greek characters on the margin of it. Before Cupid handed her glass to Erato, he just touched it with his own lips. Then he sat down by Erato's side, playing with her long hair. "Erato," he said, "I would like to wrap your beautiful dark hair all around me, and go to sleep. There's a faint scent of those yellow roses about it, and it's awfully soft and warm. I love you, Erato."

"You ought to love all of us," said Clio reprovingly.

"I try to," said Cupid, very soberly, "and it's tough work with some of them," he added under his breath.

"Cupid, darling," whispered Erato to him, "to morrow I will give you the bowstring that you wanted."

"Thanks awfully," said Cupid, "and you must tell the next story, you know, and I will lie here and listen to it. Tell me the story again about that shepherd in Sicily who——"

"Hush! hush!" interrupted Erato, "some of the sisters hardly like that kind of story; and they say that the young students at work in the colleges below us never think of love, and would not care to hear about it."

"Well," replied Cupid, with some assumption of importance, "I was there last June week on business, and I bagged three hundred and forty-two brace. That looks rather different, I fancy. Every man that I hit is engaged. They write long letters to Her. They keep faded flowers which She wore. They are beginning to drop all their bachelor friends. One of them has made a kind of little shrine on his mantelpiece, in which he keeps one tiny white satin slipper that She wore, and also a large photograph of Her. Unfortunately the virus—I mean the sweet influence —is not always permanent. Only too often the June week of one year undoes the work of the previous June. I feel sure they would like to hear the story about the Sicilian shepherd, and how he got to the cave, and found——"

"Hush!" said Erato quickly, "that's the most dangerous part of all. We'll see about it though. Clio," she added, raising her voice, "Cupid tells me that you must be a little mistaken about those young students; he says that——"

"I am sorry to have to interrupt you," remarked Clio,

" but I have asked Melpomene to tell us a soul-moving story, and she is going to commence."

" I am not going to listen to that bloodthirsty hag," whispered Cupid to Erato. He kissed her and passed out of the room. Erato was busy with the curious little silver brazier, from which the smoke began to ascend more quickly.

Melpomene took a draught of her blood-and-seltzer, and began in a deep and husky voice :—

* * * * *

A watchman stood on a lonely tower, looking eastward, and whistling " Wait till the clouds roll by," shredding it in as a remedy against impatience. And that watchman was nothing if he was not classical.

He pondered upon the history of the house. For the master was away from home, having gone to a lonely place not marked on the maps, in order to make atonement for his crime. Ten years before he had eaten a veal-and-ham pie, in which, owing to the inadvertence of the cook, his eldest daughter had taken the place of the veal-and-ham. And the cook's carelessness had been entirely due to absence of mind: he was distraught because his son had just murdered his aunt, and the son had murdered the aunt because his mind was unhinged owing to a sudden depreciation in nitrates, which he had bought largely. And the gods had caused the nitrates to depreciate because one of the directors hadn't sacrificed anything except one thigh slice, rather fat, for the last two years. And the director hadn't sacrificed anything else, because he got his butcher's meat under contract and the butcher had bilked him. And the butcher had been

compelled to bilk him, because the gods had sent a
murrain on all the cattle in the world, to punish one pig
that they had a spite against. This was not quite the
ordinary curse, descending from father to son with the silver
spoons and the mortgages. It went zigzag, like a snipe.
Many people had taken snap-shots at it with sacrifices, but
they hadn't been able to stop it. Nobody knew where that
curse was going to next; so a general interest in it prevailed. Teiresias had taken a long prayer at it, just as it
was hopping from the director to the cook's family, and
missed badly. And now the master of the watchman's
house — by name Eustinkides — had fired a ten-years'
penance at it. Some thought he'd hit it; others said it was
lying low, and would get up again in a minute.

This distressed the watchman. He felt uneasy. It was
one of those frisky curses, with an everlasting ricochet about
it, going on like sempiternal billiards with a bad cushion.
He did not think it probable, of course, that it would hit
him. He was in such a very humble position in life. But
still he would have felt more comfortable if he could have
seen that curse getting to work somewhere else. It was not
a pleasant thing to have hanging about the house. In
the meantime he awaited the coming of Eustinkides. The
master had ordered that at the moment when he appeared
in sight the hot water should be turned into the bath.
For, during the ten years' penance in the place not
recognised by the Atlas, he had carefully abstained from all
manner of washing, and had not so much as breathed the
name of soap. Suddenly the watchman removed his eye
from the telescope, and cried : " Listen, ye that are within
the house. For on the road is a curious geological forma-

tion that walks, and a staff is stuck in a projecting portion of one of its upper strata." When it came nearer, and within hearing, the watchman called out to it:

"What ho! old alluvial deposit. How's your ammonites?"

A deep voice answered: "I am thy master, Eustinkides."

"Oh! sorry!" gasped the watchman, and disappeared abruptly. Whish! The hot water poured into the bath.

An hour afterwards Eustinkides lay in that bath, and soaked. As fragments of other climates slowly detached themselves from him, he thought of his penance and of his journey home. He had stopped at Delphi and put himself in communication with Zeus. "Could you tell me how to stop this curse, Mr. Zeus?" he called up the communication tube. He waited for some little time, and then a hollow voice replied:

"One pork chop and mashed. Two in order." At this Eustinkides had at first been angry; but afterwards it seemed to him that it might be a mystery. He thought of writing to Zeus to ask for a further explanation, but there was the difficulty about the address. He felt sure it would not do to write:

—— Zeus, Esq.,
Up Top, R.S.O.

So he dried himself slowly, and went into the study. As he sat there, his French cook was announced, to consult with him on the question of dinner. While they were talking, a smell came out of the kitchen and walked slowly upstairs; it was a strong young smell, but it was lazy. It lounged into the study, and sat down under the King's nose.

"Ah!" said Eustinkides, "that is very pleasant. What is that you are cooking downstairs?"

"Pork chops for myself and the watchman," said the cook.

In a moment the words of the oracle flashed across into the mind of Eustinkides. "I also will eat pork chops, but they must not be cut from the animal whereof my servants eat. So go out, and catch another pig, and kill him, and chop him, and cook him, and bring me the result."

So the cook went out, and caught a butcher who was very careless, and demanded a pig. And the careless butcher remembered that he had killed a pig a month or two before, but he had entirely forgotten what he had done with it. At last he found it in the coal-cellar, and brought it to the cook. "It's a bit dusty," he remarked, "but that'l, all wash off."

"There's something wrong with that pig," said the cook as he prepared dinner for Eustinkides.

"There's something deuced wrong with these chops," remarked Eustinkides as he worked his way slowly through them. However, he felt sure that he was doing the right thing, and carrying out the commands of Zeus, so he did not much mind at the time.

A quarter of an hour afterwards he staggered into a chemist's. "Give us two-pennyworth of any quick sort of death, will you?" he gasped faintly.

"What are you suffering from?"

"Cursed pork," he murmured.

That was precisely it. The pig from which those chops had been taken was the very pig which the gods had such a spite against. Eustinkides was carried home to fulfil his destiny. His last words were : "Apple sauce !"

So the front end of the curse run into the hinder end, and that smashed the thing up. Wherefore let us all reverence the name of Eustinkides, and refrain from soap and sin.

*　　*　　*　　*　　*

Melpomene fainted, and squirmed on the floor. I cannot say that I was surprised. They picked her up, and gave her a little more blood-and-seltzer, and she recovered gradually.

"Tragedy *does* take it out of one," she explained.

"There isn't any more of the story, is there?" asked Thalia.

" No, that's all."

" Thank Zeus !" all the sisters ejaculated fervently, but in a whisper.

V.

CLIO was toying with the delicate little glass from which she had been drinking. "Before we have the next story, one of you might sing something," she said. "I shall be glad to play the accompaniment on the sackbut, which is a historical instrument. We first hear of it as being in use about the latter end of the——"

"Let's see," said Erato, shamelessly interrupting, "I was to tell the next story, I think."

"Well, let's have the song first."

"I like music at night," said Erato. "At night it has a speaking voice, and one understands it better. And it would be a good introduction to my story; but it must not be a drawing-room song. They are called drawing-room songs because they are whistled in the street. No, my song must be good. There mustn't be any—

> Love me! love me forrever!
> Till the years shall porse awye
> Beside the flowin' river
> You 'ear the words I sye.

> Love me! love me forrever!
> Love, though the world grows cold,
> Till no more we roam, and they call us 'ome.
> And there's tew more lambs in the fold.

That sort of thing couldn't possibly make anybody love anybody, you know. It's rather queer," she continued meditatively, "but one goes out at night all alone, and it's quiet, and a lot of little stars show you how big the darkness is. You're thinking just about ordinary things; and without any reason there comes into your head a bit of one of the Nocturnes—Chopin's, the eleventh, I think—and straightway you feel as if you'll die unless you kiss somebody you're awfully fond of. And, of course, being alone, you can't. And so you get sorrowful. It's queer, because there's nothing about love in all that—the music, and quiet, and darkness—to make one think about it; but one always does—at least I do."

"My dear Erato!" remonstrated Clio.

"Well, I do. Euterpe shall sing to us now. I don't mind a song that can be sung in a drawing-room—it's the drawing-room song that I hate. But Euterpe knows all about it, and she sings beautifully, and she's very pretty—and yet she's shy."

Erato was quite shameless in her favouritism. But she had chosen well. Euterpe was shy and quiet, but she loved singing. She smiled at Erato, and seated herself at a cottage piano in one corner of the cloud-room. I had not noticed before that there was a piano. She refused Clio's offer to accompany her on the sackbut, and another offer from Terpsichore to accompany her on the banjo. She was quiet, but when it came to music she was firm. The music of her song was beautiful, but owing to the expense of printing music it is cheaper to give the words :—

Down the dusty road together
  Homeward pass the hurrying sheep,
Stupid with the summer weather,
  Too much grass and too much sleep.
I, their shepherd, sing to thee
That summer is a joy to me.

Down the shore rolled waves all creamy
  With the flecked surf yesternight ;
I swam far out in starlight dreamy,
  In moving waters, cool and bright.
I, the shepherd, sing to thee
I love the strong life of the sea.

And upon the hillside growing,
  Where the fat sheep dozed in shade,
Bright red poppies I found blowing,
  Drowsy, tall, and loosely made.
I, the shepherd, sing to thee
How fair the bright red poppies be.

To the red-tiled homestead bending
  Winds the road, so white and long ;
Day and work are near their ending,
  Sleep and dreams will end my song.
I, the shepherd, sing to thee ;
In the dream-time answer me.

"Dear Euterpe," said Erato, "you must have been thinking of Sicily. It brings it all back to my mind, how he and I——" Erato paused. "Clio," she said at last, "I don't want to tell the next story. Let one of the others tell it. Perhaps I sha'n't listen very much, but you must forgive me. I want to lie here, and think, and think, with music in my head."

"Perhaps Polymnia has a story to tell us," suggested Clio.

Polymnia wore a long robe of pearly-grey; her face was pale, and her eyes were deep and thoughtful.

"Yes," she said, in a low musical voice, "I remember a story."

And this is the story which she remembered :—

* * * * *

It happened one day that Zeus was in a bad temper—a thoroughly bad temper. When this took place the whole of Olympus knew it. John Ganymede knew it. He had grown respectable and middle-aged. He was inclined to be portly, and still more inclined to give his views on anything to anybody. Just at present he was standing in his pantry, polishing glasses, and talking to the Deputy Cloud-controller.

"There's no pleasin' of him, when he's like that," said Ganymede, shaking his bald respectable head. "Last night he was suthin' awful. 'Ganymede,' he says to me, when I brings him his whisky last thing afore he goes to bed, 'you can pour it out for me.' So I does. 'And you can put hot water in it.' So I does again. 'I think a couple of lumps of sugar would improve it—and a little bit of lemon peel—don't you, Ganymede?' 'Yessir, suttinly sir,' I says, and puts 'em in. 'Grate a little nutmeg on the top.' I were surprised, o' course, but I did it. 'Stick a couple of spoonfuls of Maraschino into it.' All this time he's lookin' as quiet and gentle as a hangel. There wasn't no Maraschino, and I had to go down to the cellar and fetch it. I measures it out careful, and says nothing. 'I'll have a large lump of ice in it, and two straws.' I thought his poor 'ead must be going, but it wasn't my place to make no remarks. I just carries out the horder. 'Have you done all that, Ganymede?' he asks, drowsy-like. 'Yessir, suttinly sir,' says I. 'Well, there,' says he, 'you—several blanks— now you can run round, and see if you can find a dog that's such a Zeus-forsaken fool as to drink it—because I ain't going to.' And with that he goes off into his bedroom, screamin' an' laughin' an' swearin' like a maniac. Now that ain't no way to be'ave."

The Deputy Cloud-controller could sympathise. That very morning Zeus had sent for him, and demanded:

" How's the wind ? "

" Due East," said the Deputy.

" Then make it due West."

The Deputy bowed, retired, and made it due West. In ten minutes' time he was summoned before Zeus again.

" Make it East and West and South and North all at once," said Zeus.

" I can't," said the Deputy.

" Then consider yourself discharged," roared Zeus.

" Then consider *yourself* a blighted idiot," replied the Deputy indiscreetly, getting ready to dodge a thunderbolt.

"So I do," said Zeus, who never was very expected. "Go away, and send me some one else to be angry with. You're stale."

The Deputy Cloud-controller had found some difficulty in getting any one to go.

"What am I to do, Mr. Ganymede?" said the Deputy despairingly. "They all say that it's more than their lives are worth. And the females won't stand his language. I must send some one, or I shall get discharged in real earnest."

"Well, pussonally," said Ganymede, "I should be very glad to oblige you, but leave this 'ere glass and plate I can't. Now, there's the Clerk of the Curses. He's pretty tough. Why don't you send him?"

"So I would," said the Deputy, "but he's away on his holiday."

"Then there's the Earth-child," suggested Ganymede, looking a little ashamed of himself.

No one quite knew how the Earth-child had come among the gods. There must have been a mistake somewhere; it was pretty generally known that she was to have been born in Arcadia. There was something of a scandal about it, too. But there she was, generally petted and liked, and happy enough among the gods.

"Yes, there's the Earth-child," said the Deputy, and he too looked a little ashamed of himself. They talked together a little while longer, and then the Deputy went away, suffering badly from conscience.

A few minutes afterwards the Earth-child walked fearlessly into the hall where Zeus was seated. She had red hair, and an intelligent face. She was bright, and affectionate, and twelve years old, and not afraid of anything.

"I heard you wanted to be angry with me, Zeus," said the child.

Zeus looked at her grimly. " I should prefer something rather bigger."

" Why do you want to be angry ? " the child asked.

" Because I've done everything, and know almost everything, and I'm quite sick of everything."

" Music ? " suggested the child.

"Sick of it!"

"Love?"

"Everything—everything, I tell you," said Zeus hastily. "I'm tired of eating, drinking, loving, hating, sleeping, walking, talking, killing—everything."

"I'm sorry for you, Zeus," said the child, with a sigh. "Couldn't you die?" she suggested afterwards, seriously.

Zeus frowned. "No, no—not that," he said. There was a moment's pause. Zeus was thinking; and, as he thought, his face grew very ugly. He was immortal, but to a certain extent his immortality was conditioned. He might die at any moment he chose, and remain dead for an hour. If at the end of that hour any one would put his lips on the lips of Zeus, and draw in his breath, then Zeus would come back to life, and he that so drew in his breath would die. But if no one did that, then Zeus himself would be dead for ever. Zeus had never ventured on the experiment; he knew that no one loved him enough. But he might play on the simplicity of the child. And take her life? No, he could not do that. But he would ask her.

"Earth-child," he said, "will you do something for me?"

"Yes, Zeus—anything that will make you happy again."

It was horribly tempting. Should he try this one thing of which he knew nothing, of which he was not tired? Yes, he must.

"I am going to sleep," he said rapidly. "I will turn this hour-glass here, and when the last grain of sand is running out, you must put your lips to mine and draw in your breath. Then I shall wake up again, and be happy."

The child stared at him with wondering eyes. "I will do it," she said.

A minute afterwards Zeus was lying dead, and the child was watching him, and in the hour-glass the sand was running out slowly. Time passed, and the child, as she watched, saw that his face was changing queerly. It was not quite like the face of one who slept. Suddenly she crept to his side, and put one hand over his heart. It was motionless. "Zeus!" she called, in a loud whisper. He did not answer, and she knew then that he was dead.

"But shall I wake him?" she said, watching the running sand.

As the last grains ran out, she bent over him, and did what he had said. He sat up with a gasp, and a look of horror died slowly out of his face. And the child lay prone on the floor, face downwards.

Zeus hardly thought of her. "Take that away," he said to Ganymede, who entered the hall just then. Ganymede went pale to the lips, but he lifted the white burden in his arms, and carried her out. "I wish we hadn't sent her," he sighed to the Deputy Cloud-controller; "I would have gone myself, if I'd known."

"I wish you had," said the Deputy. "Both of us together are not worth her."

Zeus had forgotten her. He could think only of the things he had known in that horrible hour. "I will never die again," he said to himself; and for many nights he could not sleep.

*   *   *   *   *

"The weather's rainy," said the Muse of Astronomy, who had drawn a curtain back and was looking out.

"Yes, but Urania," murmured Terpsichore, knowing it was wrong, but quite unable to help it.

VI.

CALLIOPE'S STORY : THE LAST STRAW.

I F Euterpe had happened to have been born a pronoun, she would not have been demonstrative or personal. She would have been self-possessive. With all her shyness, she had herself perfectly in hand. She always was a little in love with somebody, but that was a secret she never told herself. Some gentle reason guided all that she did. And now for some little time she had been watching Erato, who was stretched in her favourite attitude on the floor of the cloud-chamber.

Now Erato had not even pretended to pay the slightest attention to Polymnia's story. She was thinking—and thinking. She thought easiest when she was lying on her back. Her hands were clasped behind her head, and she looked upwards with wide-opened eyes. You never saw such eyes. They told one half the story, how—with all her waywardness and petulance and laughter—love was the life of her. And now, as she lay dreaming, it seemed that it was noon in Sicily, and the flocks were sleeping; and he rested in the shade—he, the shepherd—singing. And now, again, the noon had passed and the night had fallen; in the dim cavern the air was fragrant and cool; one heard no footsteps on the thin white sand; she said

nothing to him, nor he to her, for all was said and sleep
was near; only for a little while they listened, and heard
the great sea singing its song eternal. And it all was over
and gone. For the gods are dead, and the steam-roller
goes about the streets ; and we are all either brutes or prigs,
and most of us are both, and there is no more love-making.
I, of course—a spiritual nature, very highly civilised—can
see that we live in an age of progress and omnibuses, and
can be thankful for it. But Erato, poor child, did not
take many things seriously—only love and the service of it.
And it happened, every now and then, that some such fit
of despondency or fierce sorrow would capture her as had
captured her now. Of late this had been happening too
often. To-night it was the song which Euterpe had sung
that had set her pondering—now thrilling her with some
exquisite recollection, now saddening her as she thought of
the present time, the epoch of the brute and the prude. It
was half-pitiful to watch, as Euterpe was watching, and to
see the laughter all die away from those red lips, and the
eyes grow liquid and suddenly close, and the tightening of
the little hands, and the hurried breathing.

Euterpe was not demonstrative. So it was the more
to her credit that she left her place, and sat down on the
cushions by Erato's side. She did not say anything to her.
She only did one or two of those gentle things that a girl
will do—a touch of the hand—a caress. And suddenly
Erato buried her head in Euterpe's lap, and clung to
her and sobbed quietly. I suppose Euterpe had the
sympathetic way. Some dogs have it: you are sitting
before your fire, alone, smoking, thinking of your bills or
your badness, or anything unpleasant, and you murmur

a few bad words; the big dog gets up, shakes himself, and thrusts his cold nose into your hand and whines dejectedly. Then you have to slap his back genially, to make him see that it is not his fault.

I do not think Clio can have noticed what had happened, for she said briskly:

"And now, Erato, we will have your story. The young men in Cambridge must be all in bed and asleep, so it won't hurt them. You must not spoil it by leaving anything out. Let it be the story of you and the shepherd, you know—and don't——"

"Clio, Clio," said Euterpe quickly, "can't you see that Erato is ill? Please go on quickly, and let Calliope tell her story. When that is finished, Erato will be all right again. She has been worrying herself."

It was not often that Euterpe said so much, and so authoritatively. Her eyes were bright: almost there were tears in them.

"I should be glad to recite to you," said Calliope, "a poem in thirty-five cantos, with two thousand stanzas to the canto, heroic metre, classical subject——"

"Swivel-action and no escapement," Thalia went on, under her breath.

"I am afraid," said Clio, "that we shall not have time for all that, much as we should like to."

"Oh, quite so," added Terpsichore, a little maliciously.

"If you would read us the synopsis now," suggested Clio.

"Or the index," said Thalia.

"Or even the advertisements at the end," Terpsichore proposed.

"I will read you no poem whatever," said Calliope severely. "*You are not—not yet ripe for it.*"

"Yes, we are very crude," sighed Thalia to Terpsichore.

"I will tell you instead a perfectly true story, quite unadorned and not at all epic. When you get a little riper, I will read you one of my own poems, but not to-night. To-night you have to put up with the following drivel."

This is the drivel which they had to put up with :—

    ✻   ✻   ✻   ✻   ✻

There was once a man, an Athenian, who was the opposite of all that he wanted to be. The gods had made him for a joke, and a very good joke he was; but as a man he was a failure.

To start with, he desired to have a perfect body and then to despise it. He wanted to be beautiful, and strong, and think nothing of it. Yet he thought a good deal of the bent piece of ugliness which was the nearest he could do to a perfect body. For he had nothing he wanted, and could do nothing he wanted. Sometimes he made good resolutions and tried to lead a fine life; then the gods dug one another in the ribs, and rolled about Olympus gasping with laughter. They knew very well that they had taken unusual pains about that man's physical composition; they had afflicted him with several hereditary taints; they knew that he might make enough good resolutions to pave the whole of— well, Westminster Abbey, and that it was a physical impossibility that he should keep any of them. "Let this man," one of the gods had said to Zeus, shortly before the failure was born, "be cowardly, sensual, and brutal." Then Zeus said that he was tired of making that sort. "Oh," the other god urged, "but we'll give him at the same time the

emotions and aspirations of a noble mind. Then we shall
see soul and body fighting, and the soul will get thrashed
every time." " Now, that *is* something like sport," Zeus had
remarked, as he gave the necessary order.

So this man went on providing amusement for gods and
men until he was twenty-five years of age. Sometimes he,
unfortunately, was quite unable to laugh at himself. Then
he wrote verses. At other times he laughed at himself
very well—often in self-defence, because it made other men
let him off easier—and then he would tear his verses up.

On that last day he lay in bed in the morning and
shivered. He had slept for a little while—he had seen to that
before he went to bed—but he was wide awake now, and
his head was burning, and his thoughts were of the kind
that tighten the muscles of the body and are likely nowadays
to lead on to padded rooms. For the day before he had
been found out; one act of fatal cowardice on his part—
such cowardice as no one could forgive—had cost a girl her
life, and this girl was the sister of his own familiar friend.
There was plenty of variety about his thoughts. Sometimes
he felt like a murderer. Sometimes he heard the dead
girl's brother speaking awful things to him, contemptuous,
heart-broken words. There was no hope of concealment,
no pretty story that he could tell. It had all been seen
and known. In his dreams that night he had been through
the whole scene again, but his own part had been altered.
In his dream he had been equal to the occasion—taken the
plunge, rescued the girl, and been welcomed with praise
and honour, and he had walked back through the streets
of Athens feeling more happy than a god. Suddenly he
awoke and recalled the facts. The girl whom he had loved

was dead—dead through his own cowardice. It was such loathly cowardice that he shuddered to think of it. All men would hate him, and yet their hatred would be nothing to his own hatred for himself. Every thought was a torture, a knife that went into his heart and brain, fiercely and with regular beat, stabbing and stabbing.

He sprang from his bed, and dressed himself hurriedly. The house seemed to him to be strangely quiet. He called—in a parched, husky voice—and no one answered. All had left him : the very slaves had run away from such a master, and he was alone. No one, he thought, would come near him now. He had served as a laughing-stock for his friends : he was now too despicable to be laughed at. If you wish the villain of your drama to be hissed as villain was never hissed before, make him during the first two acts the low comedian of the piece.

The man was trembling and shuddering. He made a small fire, and crouched down by it. Ah, if he only had it to do again ! A million deaths were better than such torture as this. An impulse—irresistible almost—came over him to shriek aloud and to tear with his hands at something. Could he be going mad ? The thought horrified him. He fetched wine, and drank it, and tried to calm himself, crouching down by the fire again. Suddenly he heard footsteps, and presently one of his old companions—and the worst man in Athens—stood before him.

" You cur ! " said his old companion.

" Leave me alone ! " gasped the crouching figure. " Leave me alone, or I will kill you."

" You know that you dare not touch me."

The coward knew it. It was true. The long knife which he had grasped fell from his fingers. "Leave me," he cried again piteously; "you can say nothing of me which I have not said of myself. You cannot hate me as I hate myself. Leave me! leave me!"

Then, with a gesture of disgust and contempt, the worst man in Athens left him. And now the strength of the wine mastered the coward, and he slept. This time dream followed dream, and every dream was cruel. It was late in the evening when he awoke. The only light in the room was that which came from the dying embers of the fire. By that light he saw to his horror the figure of a child standing there—a white-faced child, with awe in her eyes—the younger sister of the girl whose death his cowardice had caused.

"I have a message for you," she said. "As I slept this afternoon she came to me, and bade me tell you that she knows all about it, and that you could not help it; the gods made you so; for the gods are strong, and it is fitting that we should be very patient."

The crouching coward said nothing.

Then the child came quickly to him and kissed his ugly face. "I am very sorry, very sorry for you," she whispered gently; and then she crept gently away.

The coward burst into tears, and, grasping the long knife once more, staggered into an inner chamber, and drew the curtain behind him. The child's kiss was the thing that had just turned the balance. From the inner chamber there was the sound of one who fell heavily, and then all was still—very still indeed.

"The worst of making that sort," Zeus remarked,

with a jerk of his thumb in the direction of that inner chamber, "is that they so seldom last. But they are certainly funny. Personally, I sha'n't sleep for laughing to-night."

    *   *   *   *   *

"Would you mind," said Euterpe quietly, "drawing back that curtain from the front of the room? A few minutes ago Erato fainted, and I can't bring her round again. I think the cool night air might revive her."

Terpsichore drew back the curtain, grumbling to herself. "Just like her—we shall have the whole place turned into a regular hospital again, I expect."

VII.

THALIA'S STORY: THE CAMEL WHO NEVER GOT STARTED.

ERATO soon recovered consciousness, although she
did not regain the spirit which she had shown at
the commencement of the evening. She leaned, white and
listless, on a pile of cushions. Cupid had brought her
water to drink; and now he waited, seated on the floor, his
knees drawn up to his chin and his hands clasped over
them, gazing lovingly and sadly at his dear Erato, or down-
ward in sheer dejection at the mosaic. Euterpe, at Erato's
request, had gone to the piano. For some time she sat
playing nothing in particular with great feeling and much
expression; but she went songwards in the end, as she
always did. As far as I can remember the words, they
were something like this—it is called "Malcontent":

At Somerset House in the noontide hour, and close to the roar of the
    Strand,
The kind policeman looks to the sky with a piece of bread in his hand,
And the pigeons all come fluttering down, because they understand.
        Would that I might a pigeon be,
        For some one on earth to care for me!
                Heigh-ho!

And when they've had enough of crumbs they turn and fly away,
Upward and onward through the smoke, and they see the city grey,
Like a rotten peach that is stuffed with flies on a stifling summer's day.
        Had I but wings I would fly afar,
        Where no disgusting cities are.
                Heigh-ho!

But the waiter brings the bill of fare and spreads it in front of me,
And pigeon-pie at one-and-four's the first thing that I see ;
Imagine what the effect of this on my young soul must be.
Almost I would that I had died,
And were under the crust with my feet outside !
Waly ! Waly ! Waly !

"These verses," said Euterpe in apology, "were written by a young man in London, who was forced to live in town, but would have preferred to have driven the cows to pasture, and to have made wreaths of buttercups to twine in his beautiful hair."

"Had he beautiful hair ?" asked Erato softly.

"N-no ; that was the difficulty," answered Euterpe.

Then she came and sat by Erato again, blushing at having spoken so much. And Erato made a good deal of her, as she always did.

"I am quite well again now, Euterpe," she said.

"Ah !" sighed Euterpe, "but this happens every night."

"Every night you swoon away," added Cupid.

"But I am quite well now, and I will never be ill any more."

"Then," said Clio, "perhaps you would tell us your story now. Love stories suit the small hours."

I am afraid Clio had wanted to hear that story all the time. But she was the incarnation of outward propriety, and had struggled against her wishes. And now it was Erato who was unwilling.

"I can't," she said in a low voice. "I could have done it before—earlier in the night—but now it reminds me of too many things."

"Then," said Clio rather snappishly, "I will ask Thalia."

Thalia had a good-humoured smile, and a very pleasant voice, but her story was nothing more than the following :—

    *   *   *   *   *

There was once a camel who had got sick of the menagerie business. And this was pardonable, because the menagerie had now been on tour for six weeks, and the trombone in the band had been out of tune all the time. There were other things that made the camel weary. The untamed tigress had a bad cough, and kept him awake at night. The showman had called him the ship of the desert at each performance, and he wanted to be called something else for a change. On one occasion he had been lying in motionless dignity, and a little boy in a tight suit had asked if he was stuffed. He had been kicked by his keeper, ridden by children, starved by the manager, and jested upon by young men with penny cigars, who sucked intermittent oranges and called one another Chollie. He was sick of the menagerie business, and he wanted to get out of it. So he made himself disagreeable. As he was passing the band-stand one night, he reached out his great neck and ate the trombone part to "Nancy Lee." This made him want to be a sailor and sing "heave-ho" during the rest of the term of his natural life. But where was the sea? He'd got no sea. He hadn't an notion, as people say. So he gave up his mind to being disagreeable again. He knocked down a beautiful child with golden hair, and trod on her, so that she died ; and the management had to send her parents a gratis admission before they'd stop grumbling. Then the camel took up his position in front of the lion's den, and said sarcastic things to the lioness. This enraged her ; and not being able to reach the camel, she ate a portion of the lion-tamer, to show her spirit. Finally he walked up to one of the elephants who had a dummy tusk, and did a little comic dentist business, insomuch that the audience jeered at the showman, and the showman said several things which were not set down in the printed guide to the show. That night the camel kicked his keeper, out of reciprocity, and then talked very high talk indeed in the still midnight hours to a hyena who had seen the world.

"I am going away," the camel said, with a pathetic gasp which was the nearest he could do to a sigh. "My soul is being stifled—quite stifled—in this place."

"That's the bread," said the hyena decidedly. "We get nothing but bread."

"It's *not* the bread," snapped the camel. "It's the smell, and the low social status of the audience. I am going to seek peace and culture in another clime. I am not happy here; there can be no true happiness in a tent which smells of thirty-four distinct species, and penny cigars on the top of them."

"Well, I hope you'll find them—the peace and culture. I'm not much on pilgrimages myself, but I believe the first thing to do is to get started. Start away."

"I will," said the camel. So he wandered slowly out of the tent, and was fetched quickly back again, and tied up, and treated with ignominy. He tried it again on the following night, and was kicked till he was more grieved than he could express. He tried it a third time, and then the menagerie management sold him to a circus.

Now, at the circus, the camel was at first exceedingly proud, because he walked in the procession, and cab-horses shied at him ; but afterwards he grew very lonely, for want of other wild beasts with whom he might converse. But at last the circus people bought an ostrich that was very cheap because it had consumption, and the camel's heart was lightened. Now the ostrich was a great romancer, and told stories of passion and bulbuls, of rivers and deserts. And the camel listened to all these stories with glowing eyes.

"I once," he said confidingly, "was going to start on a pilgrimage to find culture, but I was prevented. And after all it would surely be better to return to my old home in the desert and taste the sweets of domesticity." Now the camel had been born in the menagerie, and knew nought of the desert, but he was nothing if he was not a talker.

"I shall lie under the palm-trees, and crop the cocoa-nuts ; plunge into the hot white sands for air and exercise ; and I shall take a wife, and she shall build herself a nest, and sit in it, and lay eggs in it."

"My dear sir !" said the ostrich with a blush.

"And then my family will gather round me in the winter evenings, and we shall play round games, and go to bed early, and regularly enjoy ourselves."

"When do you start on your pilgrimage in search of domesticity ?"

"I shall start, wind and weather permitting, to-morrow at one p.m."

But he did not start then, because he ate of circus bread, which was so exceedingly diseased that he fell on a bed of sickness. And the circus company saw that he would die, and advertised him for sale very cheap. And he was bought by an ardent young curate who had an enthusiastic but indistinct idea that the poor beast might be utilised to illustrate a lecture on the Holy Land.

Now the curate was a very humane man, and lodged the camel meanwhile at a livery stable. And while he was writing a sermon against all manner of pride, that night a message came to him from the livery stable to say that the camel had very bad spasms, and had kicked a large hole in the ostler. The curate, from force of habit, sent the poor quadruped a pound of tea, a bottle of port, and a tract called, "Mother's Mangle; or, Have you a Penny for the Ticket?" The ostler drank the port, and the camel ate the tea. So much tea made him very nervous, and out of compassion they put a cat in the stable to keep him company.

"Pleased to meet you," said the cat. "Will you sing something?" The cat knew perfectly well, of course, that camels cannot sing; it wanted to make the animal return the polite inquiry, and so get a chance of letting off an erotic song which it had learned in the stables. But the camel was not such a fool as that.

"I dislike music," he said. "I went in search of culture, and never got started. I also went in search of domesticity, and never got started. I am now going on a third pilgrimage,—but it will not be in search of music."

"Do you like milk?" said the cat rather inconsequently.

"No," said the camel.

"Do you like being scratched under the left ear?"

"No," said the camel.

" Can you catch mice and kill them slowly ? "

" Look here," said the camel, now justly irritated, "you're not the Catechism, and you're not the Census ; what's the point of all these questions ? "

" I was going," replied the cat, rather aggrieved, "to suggest some object for your pilgrimage, and I wished to see what you liked."

" Well, if that's all," said the camel, " I've quite made up my mind. I am going to search for death. I shall start, if the tide serves, at six a.m. to-morrow morning."

But he didn't, because he died that night. And as he arrived without ever starting, it has been argued by some that he must have been a genius. If he had stuck half-way without ever arriving, he would have been only a camel of considerable talent.

But these things may be otherwise. Things generally are.

*   *   *   *   *

" Has that story got an inner meaning ? " asked Terpsichore.

" Yes," said Thalia.

" What is it ? "

" Don't know," said Thalia.

" If you do know, you ought to say," remarked Clio.

" I do not think the story is quite—quite—well, you know."

" No, I don't," said Thalia.

" Nor do I," said Terpsichore.

They were just going to quarrel a little more, when Euterpe exclaimed : " Look, Erato, the dawn is breaking ; it is already a little lighter in the East." She added gently, after a pause, " Don't you think you had better go to bed now, Cupid ? "

" No, no," said Cupid, " I want to stay with my darling Erato. I love you, too, Euterpe, but I love Erato more than anything else in the whole world."

" Then come and kiss me—again, and again," said Erato.

VIII.

"YES," said Clio, "it will soon be morning. There will be time only for one more story. Urania shall tell it to us. Do you not think that you had better go and rest now, Erato? You look so tired."

"I am tired," answered Erato, "but it is not the tiredness that wants sleep. And I should like to hear Urania's story." She was very pale; dark shadows lay under her burning eyes; her face seemed spiritualised. Her ways and her voice were subdued and gentle now. The brightness and vivacity were gone. Sometimes she would look lovingly up into Euterpe's eyes, or touch caressingly Cupid's curly hair. For the most part she lay motionless, and seemed to be looking fixedly at something—some vision unseen by her sisters.

But Cupid never ceased to look earnestly at her, with trouble on his pretty, boyish face. And all of them felt the strange nervous tension of those who have watched far into the night; an excited tremor came over them, bringing with it flashing, vivid imaginings. There was a pause, a silence that was like a prayer to the dawning light. Then Terpsichore arose, with no merriment, as of old, upon her face, but a look of eager penitence. And she knelt down by Erato's side, and whispered—so softly that only Erato might hear it—"Forgive me, Erato, forgive me! I did not love you once as well as I love you now. I was half jealous because you seemed to like Euterpe better than you liked me, and because you were so beautiful. But I do love you now—I love you more than I can say. Oh, forgive me, Erato!"

Erato kissed her on the lips, and Terpsichore went back to her place, crying a little, for no particular reason, and hoping that no one noticed it, after the manner of maidens.

Suddenly Urania spoke, with a deep thrill in her voice. This was her story :—

    •   •   •   ,   •

There was once a man who was very careful. He saluted the sun, spoiled a good floor by making libations, sacrificed freely, and learned by heart what enabled him to remember the distinction between the *dies fastus* and the *dies nefastus*. In fact, he did all that could be done. And his number in the books was number one hundred and three.

Now, at the end of the quarter, Zeus & Co. were going through their books. It was wearying work and dry work. Ganymede was in and out of the office all day with liquors, and Mercury had been run off his legs with messages to the different departments. The clerk was reading out the items in a dreary monotone.

"Number one hundred and one. Dead. Cholera."

"That was a capital cholera," murmured Co., "and did its work well. Go on, clerk."

"Used to live in Eubœa. Killed to spite his sister, because she——"

" That'll do," said Zeus hurriedly ; " I remember that case —a stupid woman, a very stupid woman—but pretty. Next, please."

" Number one hundred and two. Philosopher still living because he wants to die."

" Say ' usual formula' when we come to that. It's no good wasting time. Has number one hundred and two got anything unpleasant the matter with him ? "

" No, sir."

" Ah, then—let me see—we'll give him a couple of ulcers. Mercury, just look in at the Punishment Department, and order a couple of large ulcers to be sent to number one hundred and two, and look sharp back. Next, please."

" Number one hundred and three. Living and prosperous. Regular in his righteousness. Further details at the Virtue Record Department."

" We ought to give that man some other reward," said Zeus, who sometimes suffered from a slight twinge of justice in damp weather.

" I'm not so sure of that," said Co., who was very healthy, and never got a touch of justice in any weather. " I hate a man who does everything right. It's so infernally hypocritical. Besides, it shows a commercial mind. He only does it in order to get something by it. I hate a commercial mind. I'll guarantee he doesn't do it out of affection for us."

Zeus sniggered. " Well, well," he said, "affection, you know, affection——" But here he was interrupted by the arrival of Mercury.

" Just look in at the Virtue Record," said Co., " and

bring the detailed list for number one hundred and three."

Mercury was back again in a minute. "The Virtue Record office is shut, sir, nobody ever virtuous after lunch, sir—shuts at one, sir. The clerk's gone home and taken the keys."

"Well," said Co., "it doesn't matter. The man is obviously a hypocrite, and he's got no business to try and make bargains with us. I don't mind it so much myself, Zeus, but it *is* such an insult to *your* dignity."

"Do you think so?" said Zeus quickly. "Then he shall repent it. I'll teach him to call ME a pettifogging huckster. I'll teach him to try to bribe ME. I'll give him a lesson. Pass me those thunderbolts. I'll scorch, and blight, and blast——"

"Gently, gently," said Co. "We may just as well try and get a little fun out of it. We'll see who can torture best—killing barred. You shall go first."

So Zeus, who had plenty of force but very little skill, went to work in the old-fashioned way. He killed the man's relations, burned down his house, destroyed his crops, wrecked his ships, reduced him to poverty, and afflicted him with the most distressing disease that the Punishment Department had in stock. And yet the man continued cheerful, saying that the gods were just and would yet send him prosperity.

"Oh, this is sickening," said Zeus; "I can't do anything with him. Now, Co., you try."

"You've not left me much to work on," said Co.; "you've taken away all the man has, except his baby son and his belief in us. I will give him something—a little accident—fever—cerebral disorder. See? Then he kills his child—you observe?—the child whom he loves more than himself. Then I restore him to his senses again. Pretty, isn't it?"

"Yes," said Zeus, a little sulkily, "you've won, Co. What made you think of that?"

"I don't know," said Co. modestly. "It was just an idea. He could not be tortured any worse than that?"

"Oh, I don't think so," objected Zeus. "You let me try again." Number one hundred and three still lay moaning on the floor of the room.

"You can try, of course," said Co.

Zeus still stuck to the old-fashioned plan of punishing by deprivation. There was only one thing left to take away— the man's belief in the gods. So he took that.

Suddenly number one hundred and three arose. There was a chill smile on his face, and he walked out into the courtyard, and looked at the rising sun. "I was mistaken,' he said. "There are no gods. All is as it chances. Good is chance and bad is chance. Nothing matters any more. I would die if I thought anything mattered. There are no more values. It is the same thing whether I murder my son, who is dearer than life to me, or whether I give alms, or whether I eat my breakfast. I shall never be sorry or happy any more. Sorrow and happiness are vain and foolish."

So he went back to his house again, and washed his hands calmly, and broke his fast.

"Well, I never!" said Zeus.

"Ah!" said Co., "you must learn the new ways. You're behind the times."

"Very well," retorted Zeus snappishly; "you needn't

say it so loudly. I don't want all Olympus to know
that."

* * * * *

" The dawn is here ! "

It was Terpsichore who spoke. She had drawn back the
curtain that formed the front of the cloud. Below them lay
the flat fen country, with dykes, and waste places, and gaunt
lonely trees. The sunrise was beautiful as a fair dream,
sprigs of light snapping on the surface of the marshy pools
and slow streams, where the cool dawn-wind shook the
water's surface.

" And now I will go to my rest," said Clio.

" And I," said the others. " And I too." Only Erato
strove to rise and could not, and fell back, breathing
quickly.

" I have grown weak," she said, and her voice was low, so
that it could hardly be heard. " I will stay here, and rest
here, in the warm light of the sun : I am cold, strangely
cold."

Euterpe and Cupid stayed with Erato. The rest all went
into an inner room, far within the cloud. Each as she
passed Erato had some gentle word to say to her. They
had bidden Cupid come with them ; he had replied with an
angry look and a shake of the head, not trusting himself to
words.

So these three were left alone in the cloud-chamber.
Erato stretched out her little hands to the sun, and watched
the light come flickering over them. Cupid had drawn a
little apart, still watching her. At last her eyes closed.
" Euterpe," she whispered, " sing to me—sing the last
song. I am drowsy, and would sleep now." So Euterpe

went to the piano. She did not sing very well, for something seemed to be wrong with her voice—a kind of huskiness:

> All's over : fall asleep.
> There is no more to say,
> There are no more tears to shed, and no more longings dead,
> And the watch ends with the day.
> Wherefore wish or weep ?
> Close your eyes, and fall asleep ;
> And happy are the dead who sleep alway.
>
> In the fair sunlight lie ;
> And let your sad thoughts stray
> Through the golden gleams of the gate of dreams
> At the breaking of the day
> Wherefore wish or weep ?
> Close your eyes, and fall asleep ;
> And happy ——

Suddenly Euterpe stopped, and for a moment there was an awful silence in the room. Then putting restraint aside, she burst into sobs, weeping as if her heart were broken, and flung herself down by Erato's side.

" Dead ? Erato, my darling ! "

And Erato did not move or speak ; her face was very beautiful as the sunlight fell upon it. There was no sound in the room but the passionate sobbing of Euterpe.

Cupid had risen. His face, for all its boyishness, was firm, unmoved ; only a little drop of blood was on his lip where he had bitten it through. He looked once at his dead Erato ; then walked to the front of the cloud-chamber, and stared vacantly outwards. It seemed to him that rings of iron were growing tighter round his chest, and stopping his breath. A humming sound was in his ears. He did not quite know what was happening.   Flecks of light seemed to dart before his hot, dry eyes.

He had stood there a long time—he knew not how long —when he heard a voice behind him.

" Cupid ! Cupid ! you loved her too."

It was Euterpe, standing there pale and sweet, looking at him, stretching her hands towards him, the tears trembling still in her eyes.

And then, at last, flinging himself into her arms and clinging to her, he wept.   " Loved her ! loved her ! " he cried.

So Erato lay there dead, and beautiful in death, and the sun shone fiercely, because it was now day, and men were going forth to their work.

THE CELESTIAL GROCERY.

A FANTASIA.

IT is precisely one year to-day since the incidents
happened which I am going to record. Since that
time I have been waiting for developments. But no
developments have taken place. I find myself, in consequence, so completely at a loss what to do or what to think,
that I venture to state the case plainly, and to ask for
advice.

Thomas Pigge, my old college friend, had sent me a
stall-ticket for the play. It was not often that I went to a
theatre at all; and I had never sat in the stalls before.
Pigge said in his letter that he had been meaning to come
with me, but had been prevented by a sprained ankle. I
found afterwards that this was quite untrue. Pigge, as a
matter of fact, had bought the ticket by a mistake. He
had been told that *The Dark Alley* was having a great
success. About a week afterwards he saw the advertisement of *Fair Alice*, and as his memory is notoriously
weak, he confused the two plays, and ordered a ticket for
the wrong one. Soon afterwards he discovered what he
had done, and learning that *Fair Alice* was a dismal failure,
he offered his ticket first to his aunt and then to his
tailor, both of whom refused it. It was then—and only

then—-that he sent it on to me. I do not think this was very nice of Thomas Pigge. I half suspected something of the kind at the time, and I was careful to make the few words of thanks that I sent him rather cold. I do not suppose he noticed it.

When I had dressed for the evening, I rang the bell—partly to tell my landlady that she need not sit up for me, but also with the intention of letting her see that, although I lived in inexpensive lodgings, I was familiar with the mode of life of English gentlemen. She surveyed me admiringly, and asked me if I would like a flower for my button-hole. " No, thank you," I said, with a smile : " they are not worn." I noticed with pleasure that these few authoritative words had their proper effect. However, as I was walking down the Strand on my way to the theatre I saw a man, in evening dress, who was wearing a rose in his coat, and thinking that it would be safe to follow his example, I spent sixpence on a gardenia with some maiden-hair. The circumstance would be trivial were it not for its bearing on after-events.

I cannot say that I enjoyed the piece altogether. The house was by no means full. The few young men in the stalls seemed mostly to know one another, and none of them knew me. The two who came in after me had those hats that shut up ; mine was an ordinary silk hat that I had worn for a year. This fact served to make me feel more lonely. My fine sensibilities render me peculiarly liable to this sort of thing; but they also do me good service by making me notice for imitation slight shades in the manners of the best people, which those of a coarser mind entirely miss. For instance, I had observed that the habitués of the stalls generally look a little careless,—not reckless precisely,—but with an air of taking everything for granted. I copied this expression throughout the evening.

A man's surroundings have a great effect upon his character; I felt myself perceptibly refined by my presence in the stalls. My position as an under-master in a private school seemed unworthy of me. " It is not," so I thought, " the profession for a gentleman. I shall change it." I must have known perfectly well that it was impossible to change it; but it pleased me to say so to myself. My old tendencies towards economy vanished. I felt that I must have a cab to take me home. It would cost two shillings probably, but that would be better than an incongruity. My æsthetic principles positively forbade me to walk home after having sat in the stalls. So I hired a four-wheeler, as I always mistrust hansoms. " After all," I said to myself as I put up the window, " what is money? We assign a value to it, but it is relative and transitory. We don't know what anything's really worth. What is money? What is money?" The words repeated themselves over and over again, in time with the rattling of the cab,—" What is money?" Such a repetition is liable to send one off to sleep. I am not sure that I might not have fallen into a doze myself, if I had not suddenly been startled into wakefulness by the stopping of the cab. I felt certain that the man could not have driven to my lodgings in the time, but I jumped out. To my amazement I found myself in an empty street. On one side of it ran a low stone wall, on the other there were houses; the darkness hid them to a great extent; but the house at which my cab had stopped was brightly lighted up, and appeared to be some kind of a shop. There was nothing set out in the windows, but over the door were the words " Joseph, Grocer." The street itself was paved with blocks of crystal, and in the air there sounded the wildest music. I turned to my cabby, utterly at a loss as to where I was, or why I was there. He sat absolutely motionless ; his hands still held the reins, but his eyes were shut. "Now then, cabby ! " I cried, "where have you taken me to ? "

He made no answer, and gave no sign of having heard me ; but the horse turned its head and looked at me. As it did so, the music ceased.

" You're starring," the horse remarked.

I remember perfectly well that one of the young men with the shut-up hats had made the same remark about some actress, and I had then wondered what he meant. "This is very confusing," I said. " It was the cabman that my remarks were addressed to."

" Look over that parapet," answered the horse.

I could not help thinking how extraordinary it was to hear a horse speak. All my life long I had been accustomed to regard a horse as a poor dumb animal. It might, of course, be all very well in fables to——

" Shut up ! " shrieked the horse.

" I never said anything," I replied, indignantly.

" No, but you thought."

" Well, I can't help thinking."

" Can't you ? If you think like that again, I'll kick this cab to splinters. I was shod yesterday. Why can't you look over the parapet, and do as you're told ? "

I gave in. I had an indistinct idea that I was going mad,

but I walked carefully across the polished street, and leaned over the low stone wall. Certainly it was a marvellous and beautiful sight. Far down, as far as my eye could reach, there was darkness; and the darkness was strewn with myriad golden stars. I heard the horse's voice behind me : "The smallest of those is the world you've just left, and this is the world you've come to."

I knew perfectly well that this was impossible and quite unscientific, and as I leaned over the wall I formed my conclusions. I had been terribly overworked lately, and probably part of my brain had given way——

" Never had any ! " yelled the horse, and went into a roar of unmannerly laughter.

I took no notice whatever of this, but went on thinking. These delusions must have arisen from some such partial failure of brain-power. It was to be hoped that it was only temporary. Probably rest and medical advice would soon set me up again. I would step across to the grocer's, and inquire where the nearest doctor lived. As I crossed the street, I noticed that the horse was humming the National Anthem. I pushed open the door of the grocery and entered. There were counters and shelves, but nothing on them. After waiting a little while I ventured to tap on the floor with my foot. A voice from the other side of the counter said :—

" What may we have the pleasure of doing for you ? "

I looked, but I could not see any one, and I ventured to say so.

"No, you can't see me. It doesn't really matter, but I think I left it downstairs. James," the voice called to some invisible person at the farther end of the shop, "what did I do with my body? I had it only this morning."

The answer came in a boyish voice: "You left it in the cellar, Joseph, when you were packing up the nightmares."

"So I did, so I did. You're right, James."

"But," I said, "I can't see James's body either."

"No, you see James has only got one. You're very inquisitive. If you must know, his body's gone to the wash. You wouldn't have him wear it dirty?"

"I generally wash my own," I said mildly.

"Well, we don't. This is a grocery, not a laundry."

"You must excuse me," I pleaded, "I'm quite a stranger in these parts." I saw it was no good to inquire for a doctor. If the grocery was part of the delusion, as it seemed to be, it would be absurd to make the inquiry there. If, on the other hand, the grocery really existed, then probably I did not require the doctor's services. But I felt very muddled about it. "I suppose you're Mr. Joseph?" I said.

"I am Joseph, and I should take it as a favour if you would tell me with what I can serve you."

"Well," I said, "judging from the state of your counter and shelves, I don't see anything you can serve me with."

"Of course you don't see," he answered, a little snappishly. "You can't see the abstract. I'm not a grocer in the concrete. Kindly shut that door. There's a draught keeps coming down the back of the place where my neck would have been, and that's a thing I can't stand."

As I shut the door I felt more bewildered than ever. An abstract grocer was beyond me, and I said so. "What, for instance, is abstract sugar?" I asked.

"Sugar's concrete," was the reply, "and if you abstract

it, you get spanked. We've got no sugar here. If you'd like a Pure White, Crystallised, Disinterested Love, we keep that, although there's not much demand. They mostly use the coarser kinds. They say they're sweeter."

" Ah ! " I cried, " you deal in abstract nouns then."

" That's more like it. It's a clumsy way of putting it, but it's fairly right. We supply, or, to speak more accurately, we groce, all the Emotions to the Solar System, and trade's very slack just now in that branch. We are doing rather better in States of Being, and we've just got a new assortment of Deaths. Now, once for all, do you intend to buy anything ? "

I remembered with joy that I had a couple of sovereigns and some loose silver in my pocket. All my life long I had suffered from want of emotional experiences. I had always regretted the want of variety, the general flatness and dulness. If the delusion or reality—I neither knew nor cared now which it was—would only last, I was determined to gratify to the full my fine perceptions. Especially was I struck with the mention of the Pure White Love. I may confess at once that I never got on much with women. I have a natural dignity and reserve that is sometimes mistaken for nervousness. I fancy it sets women against me. Somehow I am never able to say to them quite what I want to say. I have often looked at a young girl, and thought that if she could only know me as I really was—if she could once regard me as apart from wretched circumstances, my poverty, my shabby clothes, my unfortunate reserve—she might abate something of her pretty scorn.

" Certainly, I intend to buy something," I said. " To

commence with, I should like to see some samples of that peculiar Love you mentioned."

"Dear me!" broke in Mr. Joseph. "How many more times am I to tell you? You can't *see* samples. You can feel them if you like. James!"

"Yes, Joseph," answered the boyish voice from the further end of the shop.

"Let's have some of the ' Pure White,'—look sharp."

"Right."

"Now then," continued Mr. Joseph. "Take that chair. Adopt an easy, natural position. Don't cross the legs. If you find the light too strong, you can blink the eyes once or twice, it won't make any difference. Head a little more this way. You're frowning. That's better. Now then, we're ready. Steady, please."

The light certainly was too strong. A sudden flash blinded me, and when I recovered my sight I was apparently no longer in the Grocery. I was in a dimly-lighted conservatory and the middle of a sentence. I have never been able to find out what could have been the beginning of it.

" . . . which it is not, and never was," I was saying. "I am content only to have told you, and now I relinquish you. Let this be my farewell, my good-bye to you before I sail from England. In books that we read, a man would have asked you for one clasp of the hands, or even one kiss, but I neither ask nor wish for that."

I looked up, and saw the girl to whom I was speaking. I had certainly never seen her before, but yet the figure was familiar. She sat in her white dress, shaded from the light by some tropical plant. It was with passionate and hopeless adoration that I looked at her, and yet I was full of a strange content; it seemed to be enough to have loved her. I saw that her head was slightly turned away from me, and that she was sobbing.

"I am sorry," I went on, "that I have made you cry. I want you to be happy, and I know there is only one way."

"I never knew it was going to be like this," she said tremulously.

For the matter of that, neither had I when I first ordered the first sample pure white. But it struck me as being all quite natural. Some of that peace which must come to men of a great soul, had come to me.

"Good-bye," I said. "I am not going to do anything desperate, anything that could cause you regret. It is enough for me to have loved you, and to feel that in comparison the rest of my life is one . . ."

Just as I had begun in the middle of a sentence so I ended in the middle of a sentence. The dim-lit conservatory and the maiden vanished, and I found myself once more in the Celestial Grocery.

"Do you like it?" asked Mr. Joseph's voice.

"Yes," I said, hesitatingly, "it is grand, it is sublime. But I don't think I could stand very much of it. How much is it a pound?"

"We don't sell it by the pound; we sell it by the spasm."

"Then," I said, "I'll take six spasms."

"James, six of the pure white."

"Right," said the voice of James.

For a moment I tried to recall the beautiful girl in white whom I had just seen. I wondered how my first sentence began and how my last sentence would have ended. I seemed to have walked for a while upon those heights of love that reach beyond the fires of passion, and on which lie the snows of perpetual purity. I felt that my self-respect had considerably increased in consequence. Here I was interrupted by Mr. Joseph.

"What will be the next order?"

"I have often longed," I replied, "for a little real happiness."

"Yes," said Mr. Joseph. "But that is a blend. You buy the ingredients and you blend them yourself. Unfortunately, we do not provide Incomes. We have a Literary Fame which gives great satisfaction. 'Political Success' is in considerable demand. Then there's 'Religious Exaltation'— not much asked for lately, I'm afraid. 'Requited Love' is not expensive, but we've had complaints that it doesn't wear well. Of course there's Death by Drowning, Death by——"

"Stop, Mr. Joseph," I cried, "I have no desire to die." I had already decided what should be my next experiment; for even under-masters have their ambitions. "I think," I said, "that I should rather like to try the 'Political Success.'"

Mr. Joseph took my order with alacrity, and the same process as before was repeated. Once more I seemed to have left the grocery. I was standing on a balcony, my hat in my hand, and below me in the street there was a surging mass of people. As far as my sight could reach I could see eager, excited faces upturned. I was just concluding a speech, and, as before, was in the middle of a sentence.

". . . not derogatory to the national sense—(cheers)—of what is the fittest, the truest, and the best way—(renewed applause)—of proving to those who at one time may have thought otherwise, that, in spite of all preconceived opinions, which, if they are not praiseworthy—and I do not say they are so—yet may with some show of justice—(hear, hear)—be asserted to have had their origin in a sentiment felt by humanity at large, and more especially by the English-speaking races, and to which we to-night, with the generosity of the conquerors towards the conquered—(loud cheers)—can well afford to extend our fullest indulgence. It is not only in the family but in a man's public capacity; not only by the fireside, but also beneath that fiercer light that beats upon the high offices of this nation—(loud and prolonged cheering)—not only with the . . ."

I would have given anything to have gone on a little further. I do not even know what my politics were, although I am inclined to form an opinion from internal evidences in my speech. But I never in all my life felt such a delightful sense of exhilaration, triumph, and power. When I came to, I found myself seated on the floor of the grocery, perspiring profusely.

"Oh, that was good," I exclaimed, "very good!" I picked myself up, and inquired eagerly what the price was, and how it was sold.

"It is expensive," said Mr. Joseph, solemnly, "very expensive; and we sell it in bursts."

I did not like to ask for further details. I expected that Mr. Joseph would give me a reasonable amount of credit, and with the literary fame that I intended to buy I thought that I should soon be able to pay for everything. But I thought it wise to order only two bursts of the "Political Success."

"Mr. Joseph," I said, "I hardly know what to order

next. I should like to have a price-list, and a week to think it over. I never bought anything abstract before. At present I've got only some 'Disinterested Love' and some 'Political Success'; do you think you could let me have some Literary Fame, Musical Ability, Personal Charm, Popularity, and Contentment?"

"It's a large order," said Mr. Joseph, "but we will do our best to execute it. James, will you see about those articles?"

"I will," said James.

"And when shall I have them?"

There was no answer.

"I should like to know when I can have them," I continued. "I don't want to hurry you. Any time in the course of a year would do. I can give you a reference if you like. The master of St. Cecilia's knows all about me. But as I did not imagine I was coming here to-night, I have brought hardly any money with me. However, if you would not object to taking two pounds on account——"

I pulled out my two sovereigns, and laid them on the counter. As I did so I looked up. I had ceased to be capable of surprise, or I think I should have been surprised. Before me, on the other side of the counter, stood a young girl. Perhaps I should more accurately describe her as a young angel, except that she had no wings or halo. She was dressed in some loose, white garment, which looked like the apotheosis of a night-gown. I could not say within a year or two how old she was, but she seemed to be on the verge of womanhood. Her figure was tall and slight. Her small white hands were clasped before her. Her face was, perhaps, a little wan and pale, but full of the most spiritual beauty. The expression upon it was one of sweet, calm seriousness. Her eyes seemed to be looking sadly at something far off. Her hair was long and dark, and fell loosely about her shoulders. I gazed at her a long time before I could speak.

"Mr. Joseph?" I stammered out, questioningly.

"Joseph and James," she said, in a low musical voice, "have gone downstairs to feed Joseph's body. They sent me up here to wait on you. What are these?"

She took up the two sovereigns I had placed on the counter.

"A mere trifle," I said. "I thought that, perhaps, it would be better to pay a trifle on account. If I had known that I was coming here, I would have brought more—I would, indeed."

"Will you please put them away?" she said, slowly. "They have no value. I will tell you about it soon. I have known you for a long time—known you so well."

I was entranced by her beauty, and could hardly find words to speak, but I muttered the usual commonplaces. It was very stupid of me, but I did not seem to recall her face. I did not even remember her name.

"No," she replied, "you have never seen me before. You will know my name one day, but not yet. I have watched you for years, and sometimes I have been with you. I am glad that you came here to-night, for I have often wished to speak with you."

It is possible that I may have looked a little incredulous, for she fixed her eyes full upon mine, leaning across the counter, and whispered something to me. I do not see that I am called upon to write down what she said. It was quite personal and private   If I did record it, it would probably be misunderstood.   But it answered its purpose. It made me feel that she knew me indeed, that here I had no impression to make and none to mar.   There was no longer any barrier of reserve between us.

"And at last you have come to me," she said.   "No one can overhear us; we are quite alone."

My cheeks were flushed and my voice trembled.   "You do not talk," I said, "as the women I met on earth, nor as Joseph and James did.   No earthly woman that I know would have whispered to me the things that you did."

"You are not angry with me for it?" she said.

I loved her for it, but I could not tell her so.   For a moment or two I gazed at her in a kind of rapture.   "You are very beautiful," I said at last.

"Yes; but that is not of any real consequence here. Here the body is always beautiful, because the spirit never spoils it.   Would that I could alter your nature and make it like ours!   But they told me that you would look at me as on your earth a man looks at a woman.   I do not understand that.   I do not know your way—ah, do not look at me so."

"I cannot help it; you draw my eyes towards you."

"Do not say that!" she cried, in a distressed voice. "Do not think of it.   I can think, and speak, and love when I am not in the body.   I almost wish that I had not come to you like this.   If I had been only a voice I should still have desired you."

Like most people of a shy disposition, I have an occasional access of boldness.   "Do you mean that you do not understand the kind of attraction that a woman has for a man?

Do you not know what flushed cheeks, and longing looks, and trembling voice mean? And yet I could believe that the earthly love would be possible to you."

"The lower is always possible for the higher," she said. "But that is not what I want. I long to-night to teach you the other love. But now that I am face to face with you I have no words. There are none in any language that will tell you. I want names for things of which you know nothing—things which with men and women of your world do not exist. I should feel no shame in speaking to you of it, for there is no shame in our love. Your love is full of shame. That was why at first I whispered to you. That was why I told you that no one could hear us. It was for your sake, not mine." She stopped and sighed.

" Why do you sigh? " I asked.

" Because I cannot say what I want."

" Try," I said.

" No, it is no use now. What have you been buying? "

I gave her a list of my purchases, and she went over them, as it seemed to me, a little sadly. " You have not bought the best things," she said. " But they will cost you all that you have here, one gardenia and a sprig of maidenhair."

" Is that flower really worth more than the two sovereigns that I offered you? "

"Yes, we have none here, and flowers are the only purity on your earth."

" But this will die in an hour."

"No," she said, " it would have died there, but here it will never die." As I laid it on the counter I noticed that even the maidenhair was quite fresh.

"If I had only known," I said, "I would have loaded my cab with flowers. Can I not come back again?"

"No—never."

"Then let me change the things that I have bought. They seemed high and noble, especially the White Love."

"Yes, you shall change them. You did not value the Love because it was noble, but because it made you feel noble."

"And what shall I buy for myself?"

"Nothing. If you had kept the goods that you ordered, you would have made a little flutter on an indescribably small portion of a rather insignificant world. You would have been called the great poet, the eminent statesman, and it would not have helped you any further—it would not have raised you any higher. Your nature would still have been bounded on the earth by earthly possibilities. No, you shall buy nothing for yourself. There is only one step that you can take that will bring you nearer me. There is only one thing that you can do that has a real value."

"You mean self-denial," I said. "I will obey you. I surrender all that I had bought. You shall give me instead the best thing for some one else—for whom?"

"For your own father."

I bent my head in shame. It was a subject of which I could hardly bear to speak ; but she with great tenderness, laying one of her little hands softly and caressingly on mine, dropped her voice almost to a whisper.

"Yes, for your father. My poor boy, there are no secrets between you and me. There is to be no shame between you and me. I know all. In the same asylum where your grandfather died your father now lies. His reason is gone.

A horrible darkness has come over his mind. He lies there moaning and ——"

"Stop!" I cried. "For pity's sake say no more. You are right. Give me the best thing for him."

"It shall be so," she said. "And now the end of your time here grows near. But, you have taken the first step. You and I have advanced a little further towards the sacred unity of the new love. Come, let us go and look down at the stars, and I will tell you about them."

She came round to my side of the counter, and we passed through the door together. Her bare feet trod lightly on the crystal blocks with which the street was paved. I gazed at her in an ecstasy of adoration. The cab was still standing there, and the horse looked round at us. He grinned horribly, showing his yellow fangs.

"Oh my! ain't it sweet!" he called out.

"You vulgar beast!" I said to him angrily, "if you say another word, I'll take that whip and simply flay you."

"You needn't distress yourself," he answered, "because you'll be asleep in two minutes."

I saw that she had taken no notice of the unmannerly animal. She had crossed the street, and was leaning over the low stone wall, with her beautiful head supported on one hand; I saw that my most dignified course was to follow her, and I did so.

"Yes," she said, pointing downwards with her finger, "those are the other worlds. They were put there to be a heating and lighting apparatus for the most insignificant of them—at least that is the prevalent creed, for the most insignificant. Do not believe it. On each one there is life, and for each one there is a purpose; all are part of one scheme that ——"

The horse was quite right. At this point, I rested my head on my arms as I leaned over the parapet, and went fast asleep. I can never forgive myself for it, but I was powerless to prevent it. I do not know how long I slept, but I woke suddenly. She was no longer leaning over the parapet; she stood on the pathway, gazing upwards, with a strange light in her eyes. Of course she was in the middle of a sentence. That was only part of the generally unsatisfactory nature of everything.

" ——would get new experiences, new data. You would think and imagine new things. You would know what the new love means. I can only speak to you as a woman to a man, but I do not look at you as a woman would. She would see only a poor little schoolmaster, not very beautiful, rather sleepy-headed, in a dress-suit much too tight for him. I too can see that. But I see also a life that long ago came out into the darkness hand-in-hand with mine. Had you been placed in this world, you would have known as I know; but I came here, and you were sent elsewhere. Out of the same clay the potter makes two vessels, one to honour and one to dishonour."

"And that is extremely unjust," I said.

"It would be quite impossible for you to think otherwise; but you are wrong. You will soon know that you are wrong."

"When?" I asked.

"On the day that you know my name, when the earthly love that you feel for me is changed to the new love of which it is the shadow, when we come back together, you and I, out of the darkness into the light."

" Where is the light?"

"Look upwards. There are no more stars, and above all seems dark. And the darkness flows on like a river, on and on. But the river will run dry at the last, the darkness will have passed at the last, and then we shall enter into the light."

" And now," said the voice of the unconscionable cab-horse behind us, " I will ask you to join with me in singing the last hymn on the paper."

" What on earth," I exclaimed testily, " is the point of making that perfectly idiotic remark?"

" Mere absent-mindedness," the brute answered. " I thought from the general style of the conversation that I was at some missionary meeting. That's all."

" At any rate," I said, "you need not interrupt a—a lady."

" Lady! S'help me! That high-toned, female grocer's assistant, a lady!" The beast positively shrieked with laughter. " Get into the cab, you little fool, and let's get home. There's no place like home."

I sprang at the cab, seized the whip, and determined to take my revenge. But I never got it. The agile beast waltzed round and round with amazing rapidity in the middle of the street. I struck out wildly; but though I occasionally hit the cab, I never succeeded in hitting the horse. All this time the cabman remained motionless. Suddenly the brute stopped, and backed the cab right into me. I fell down on the pavement by the low wall. I picked myself up and gazed around.

She was no longer there.

I staggered across the road. The lights were out in the

grocery. I tried the door, but it was locked. I shook it, and called loudly, but no answer came. Once more I turned savagely on the horse, but at the first stroke the whip broke in my hands.

"Now then," he yelled, "you little fool, get into the cab, and let's enter into the Light!"

For a moment I stood there helpless. I felt weak and sick with my fall. Then I flung down the broken whip, and got into the cab, which started instantly at full speed. I buried my face in my hands, and burst into tears.

When, after a moment, I looked up again, there was the roar of the London streets about me, and we were within a hundred yards of my lodgings. The cab stopped at them, and I got out. It was evident that the cabman knew nothing about what had happened; he looked cheery, comfortable, and commonplace. I saw that there would be no use in speaking to him about it. I merely paid him three times his proper fare, to compensate him for the loss of his whip, which, by the way, he did not seem to have noticed.

I was very tired, and soon went off to sleep. I had lost fame, and I had gained for my father a return to sanity. It was worth the sacrifice. He should come to London, and live with me. It was years since I had been able to speak to him. Then slumber interrupted my thoughts.

As soon as I woke in the morning I sprang from my bed, and took up my dress-coat. No, it was no dream. The gardenia and maidenhair were gone, and my father had regained his reason. Would that I could see her once more, and thank her.

There came a tap at my door.

"All right, Mrs. Smith," I cried. "I'm getting up."

"There's a telegram for you, sir."

It was pushed under the door. I opened it. It was from the doctor at the asylum where my father was placed, and it read as follows:—

"Your father died suddenly early this morning. Please come at once."

There have been no further developments, and I do not know what to do. I feel that I must see her, and ask her. I cannot understand. And, alas! I cannot get to her.

*   *   *   *   *

Since writing the above, I have had a letter from my Principal. He wants my resignation. He says something about "strangeness of manner—medical advice—real kindness to me—hope for recovery." Mrs. Smith has asked me, with tears in her eyes, to leave my apartments. She says that I have been most regular in my payments, and in every way showed myself to be a perfect gentleman; but the other lodgers are frightened of me, and I frighten her sometimes. She can feel for me, because she had a cousin who once went off like that; but would I mind going?

Well, I have resigned my post, and to-night I leave my lodgings. I am very lonely.

"BILL."

THE STORY OF A BOY WHOM THE GODS LOVED.

BILL came slowly up the steps from a basement flat in Pond Buildings, crossed the pavement, and sat down on the kerb-stone in the sunshine, with his feet in a delightful puddle. He was reflecting.

"All that fuss about a dead byeby!" he said to himself.

He was quite a little boy, with a dirty face, gipsy eyes, and a love for animals. He had slept the deep sleep of childhood the night before, and had heard nothing of what was happening. In the early morning, however, he had been enlightened by his father—a weak man, with a shuffling gait, who tried to do right and generally failed.

"Bill, cummere. Larst night there were a byeby come to be your sister if she'd grow'd. But she didn't live more'n hour. An' that's why your awnt's 'ere, an' mind yer do whort she tells yer, an' don't go inter the other room, an' don't do nothin' 'cep' whort yer told, or I'll break yer 'ead for yer, sure's death, I will!"

Then Bill's father had gone away to his work, being unable to afford the loss of a day; and Bill's vehement, red-haired aunt had come into the kitchen, and shaken

him, and abused him, and given him some breakfast.
Bill's aunt was one of those unfortunate people who cannot
love one person without hating three others to make up for
it. Just at present she was loving Bill's mother, her sister,
very much, and retained her self-respect by being very strict
with Bill's father, with Bill himself, and with the doctor.
She instructed Bill that he was not to go to school that
morning. He was to remain absolutely quiet in the kitchen,
because he might be wanted to run errands and do odd
jobs. For some time Bill had obeyed her, and then
monotony tempted him to include the little yard at the
back in his definition of the kitchen. All the basement
flats in Pond Buildings have little yards at the back. Most
of the inhabitants use them as drying-grounds. In some
of them there is a dead shrub or the remains of a sanguine
geranium that failed; in all of them there are cinders and
very old meat-tins. Now, when Bill went out into the
yard, he found the black cat, which he called Simon
Peter, asleep in the sun on the wall. Simon Peter did
not belong to anyone; she roamed about at the back
of Pond Buildings, dodged anything that was thrown at
her, and ate unspeakable things. She had formed a
melancholy and unremunerative attachment to Bill; her
name had been suggested to him by stray visits to a
Sunday-school, forced on him during a short season when
his father, to use his own phrase, had got religion.
"Siming Peter," said Bill, as he scratched her gently
under the ear, "Siming Peter, my cat, come in 'ere along
o' me and 'ave some milk."

It is not at all probable that Simon Peter was deceived
by this. She must have known that, with the best intentions

in the world, Bill could not do so much as this for her. Yet she blinked at him with her lazy green eyes, and followed him from the yard into the kitchen. Bill filled a saucer with water, and put it down on the ground before her. "There yer are, Siming Peter," he said; "an' that's better for yer nor any milk." Simon Peter put up her back slowly, mewed contemptuously, and trotted out into the yard again. Bill, dashing after her, trod on the saucer and broke it, and overturned a chair. In another moment he was in the clutches of his fierce aunt.

"Do you want to kill your blessed mother, you devil? Didn't I tell yer to sit quoite? An' a good saucer broke, with the poor dead corpse of your byeby sister lyin' in the next room. Go hout! You're more nuisance nor you're wuth. See 'ere. Don't you show your ugly 'ead 'ere agin afore night. An' when yer comes back I'll tell your father of yer, an' 'e 'll skin yer alive. Dinner? Not for such as you. Hout yer git."

So Bill had been turned out, and now sat with his feet in a delightful puddle, reflecting for a minute or two on dead babies, injustice, puddles, and other things. It was a larger puddle, as far as Bill could see, than any other in the street, and it was this which made it so charming. But a puddle is of no use to anyone who has not got something to float on it. If you have something to float on it you can imagine boats, and races, and storms, and it becomes a magnificent playground for the imagination; otherwise the biggest puddle is simply a puddle, and it is nothing more. So Bill started down the street to look for something which would float, a scrap of paper or a straw. He was stopped by a lanky unkempt girl with yellow hair, who was leaning

on a broom that was almost bald, outside an open door.
She was four or five years older than Bill, and she was
very fond of him. The girls of the wretched neighbourhood for the most part rather petted Bill; they did
so, without knowing their reason, because he was quaint,
and pretty, and little. He was rather dirty it was true,
but then so were they; and for the most part they were
not so pretty.

"Bill," said the yellow-haired girl, "why awnt yer at
school? You'll ketch it, Bill."

"No, I 'ont. They kep' me, 'cos we've got a byeby, an'
the byeby's dead. Then they tunned me out for breakin'
a saucer when I was goin' after Siming Peter what I were
feedin', an' I ain't to 'ave no dinner, and I ain't to come
back afore night, and when I do come back I'm goin' to be
walloped. I wish I was dead!"

"Oh, Bill, you *are* a bad boy; what are yer goin' to
do?"

"Play ships at that puddle. I was lookin' for sutthin'
what 'ud do for ships, an' can't find nothin'."

"An' what'll yer do about dinner?"

"I ain't goin' to 'ave no dinner," said Bill, solemnly,
"I'm goin' to starve. They don't keer. Dead byebies is
what *they* like."

The lanky girl leaned her broom against the wall, sat
down on the doorstep, and commenced the research of a
pocket; the pocket yielded her one penny.

"Look 'ere, Bill," she said, "you take this and git yourself sutthin' to eat."

Bill shook his head, and pressed his lips together. He
was much moved.

"I 'ad it give me a week ago, and I sived it 'cos there warn't nothin' what I wanted. So you take it. I don't want it. If yer like, yer can give us a kiss for it." She pressed it into his hand. "There ain't no other little boy I know what I'd give it to," she added rather inconsistently.

Bill nodded his head, and the lips grew a little tremulous. He had been treated cruelly all the morning, and this sudden change to sympathy and generosity was almost too much for him. He kissed the yellow-haired girl—once timidly and then suddenly with great affection.

"Why, Bill," she said, "I ain't done nothin' to 'urt yer, yer look ommust as if yer was goin' to cry."

"No, I ain't," replied Bill, finding words with difficulty, " but—but I 'ate ev'rybody in the world 'cep' you."

Then he walked away with great dignity, and every nerve in his excitable little body quivering. He felt on the whole rather more wretched than before. The contrast made him feel both sides of it more deeply. He had forgotten now about the beautiful puddle and his intention to play ships. He wandered down the main street, and then down a side street which led behind a grim, frowning church. And here he found something which attracted his attention. It was a dirty little shop which a small tobacconist and an almost microscopical grocer had used successively as a last step before bankruptcy. It had then remained for some time unoccupied. But now the whole of the window was occupied with one great bright picture, before which a small crowd had gathered. It represented a beautiful mermaid swimming in a beautiful sea, accompanied by a small octopus and some boiled shrimps. Her hair was very golden and very long; her eyes were very blue; she was very pink and very fat. Underneath was the announcement—

THE MERMAID OF THE WESTERN PACIFIC!

Positively to be Seen Within!!

FOR A FEW DAYS ONLY.

ADMISSION ONE PENNY

An old man was standing in the doorway, with a tattered red curtain behind him, supplying further details of the history and personal appearance of the mermaid. He looked slightly military, distinctly intemperate, and very unfortunate, yet he was energetic.

"What it comes to is this—for a few days only I am offering two 'igh-class entertainments at the price of one. The performance commences with an exhibition by that most marvellous Spanish conjurer, Madumarsell Rimbini, and concludes with that unparalleled wonder of the world, the mermaid of the Western Pasuffolk. I have been asked frequent if it pays me to do this. No, it does *not* pay me. I am doing it entirely as an advertisement. Kindly take notice that this mermaid is not a shadder, faked up with lookin' glasses. She is real—solid—genuine—discovered by a English officer while cruisin' in the Western Pasuffolk, and purchased direct from 'im by myself. The performance will commence in one minute. If any gentleman is not able to stay now, I may remark that the performances will be repeated agin this evenin' from seven to ten. What it comes to is this—for a few days only, etc."

Of course Bill had seen shows of a kind before. He had seen a 'bus horse stumble, and almost pick itself up, and stumble again, and finally go down half on the kerb-stone. That had been attractive, but there had been nothing to pay for it. Again, in his Sunday-school days, he had been present at an entertainment where the exhilaration of solid buns and dissolving views had been gently tempered by a short address. That too was attractive, but it had been free. And now it would not be possible to see this beautiful buoyant creature swimming in clear shrimp-haunted waters unless he paid a penny for it, the only penny that he possessed. Never before had he paid anything to go any-where. The temptation was masterful. It gripped him, and drew him towards the tattered red curtain that hung over the entrance. In another minute he had paid his penny, and stood within.

At one end of the shop a low stage had been erected. On the stage was something which looked like a large packing-case with a piece of red baize thrown over it. There was a small table, on which were two packs of playing-cards and a brightly coloured pill-box, and a tired fat woman in a low dress of peculiar frowziness. As the audience entered she put a smile on her face, where it remained fixed as if it had been pinned. The performance commenced with three clumsy card-tricks. Then she requested some one in the audience to put a halfpenny in the painted pill-box and see it changed into a shilling. The audience felt that they had been weak in paying a penny to see the show, and on this last point they were adamant. They would put no halfpennies in no pill-boxes. They were now firm. So also was the Spanish conjurer, and this trick was omitted. She intimated that she would now proceed to the second part of the entertainment, the exhibition of the mermaid of the Western Pacific. She removed, dramatically, the red-baize cover, disclosing a glass case. The audience pressed forward to examine its contents. The case was filled for the most part with those romantic rocks and grasses which conventionality has appointed to be a suitable setting for stuffed canaries, or stuffed dogs, or anything that is stuffed. There was a back ground of painted sky and sea ; and in the front there was a small, most horrible figure, looking straight at Bill out of hideous, green, glassy eyes. It was not the lovely creature depicted in the window outside. It was a monstrous thing, a contemptible fraud to the practised intelligence, but to Bill's childish, excitable mind a thing of unspeakable horror and fascination. The lower half was a wilted, withered fish ; then came a girdle of seaweed, and then something which was near to being human, yellow and waxy, with a ghastly face, a bald head, and those eyes that would keep looking at Bill. He shut his own eyes for a second ; when he opened them again the monstrous thing was still looking at him.

There were two men standing near to Bill. One of them was a very young and very satirical carpenter, with a foot-rule sticking out of his coat-pocket. "So that's a mermaid !" he remarked. "Yer call that a mermaid—oh !—indeed, a mermaid—oh, yes ! "

"Seems to me," said the other man, middle-aged, cadaverous, and dressed in rusty black, "that it's a sight more like a dead byeby."

"Well, you *ought* to know," replied the satirical carpenter, grinning.

Bill heard this. So in that basement flat in Pond Buildings, Bill's home, there was something lying quite still and waiting for him, to frighten him. He had never thought what a dead baby would be like. His mind began to work in flashes. The first flash reminded him of some horrible stories which his red-haired, vehement aunt had told him, to terrify him into being good. He had objected at the close of one story that dead people could not walk about.

"You don't know," his aunt had replied, " nobody knows, what dead people can do." In the second flash he imagined that he had gone home, had been lectured by his aunt, and beaten by his father, and had cried himself to sleep. He would wake up at night, when all was quiet—he felt sure of it—and the room would not be quite dark. He would see by the white moonlight a horrible, yellow, waxy thing crawling across the floor. It would not go to the right or to the left, but straight towards him. It would be his dead baby sister, and it would have a face like the face of the mermaid, and it would stare at him. He would be unable to call out. It would come nearer and nearer, and at last it would touch him. Then he would die of fright.

No, he would not go home, not until the dead baby had been taken away.

As the audience crowded out through the narrow doorway, Bill touched the man in shabby black :

"Please, sir, 'ow long is it afore they bury dead babies ? "

The man stared at him searchingly. "What do yer want to know that for? Depends on the weather partly, and on the inclinations of the bereaved party. 'Soon as possible' 's allus my advice, but they let it go for days frequent."

Bill thanked him, and walked aimlessly away. He could not get the terror out of his mind. He walked through street after street, so absorbed in horrible thoughts that he hardly noticed what direction he was taking, and only just escaped being run over. He had been wandering for over an hour when he came across two boys, whom he knew, playing marbles. This was companionship and diversion for his thoughts. For some time he watched the game with interest, and then one of the players pulled from his pocket two large marbles of greenish glass, and set them rolling. Bill turned away at once, for he had been reminded of those green eyes. He imagined that they were still looking at him; but, in his imagination, they belonged not to the mermaid, but to the dead baby. He wished again and again that he had never been to that show. He was growing almost desperate with terror. Of course, his state of mind was to some extent due to the fact that he had eaten nothing for eight hours. But then, Bill did not know this. Suddenly he gave a great start, and a gasp for breath, for he had been touched on the shoulder. He looked up and saw his father. Now Bill's father had drunk two glasses of bad beer during his dinner hour, and in consequence he was feeling somewhat angry and somewhat self-righteous, for his head was exceedingly weak and poor. He addressed Bill very solemnly—

" Loit'rin' in the streets! loit'rin' and playin' in the streets!

What's the good o' my bringing of yer up in the fear o Gawd ? "

Bill had no answer to make ; so his father aimed a blow at him, which Bill dodged.

"All right," his father continued, " I'm sent out on a jorb, and I ain't got the time to wallup yer now. But you mark my words—this very night, as sure as my name's what it is, I'll knock yer blawstid 'ead off."

At any other time this would have frightened Bill. But now it came as a positive relief. There is no fear so painful, so maddening, as the fear of the supernatural. The promise that he should have his head knocked off had in itself but little charm or attraction. But in that case he knew what to fear and from whence to fear it. It took his thoughts away for a few minutes from the horror of that dead baby, whose ghastly face he pictured to himself so clearly. But it was only for a few minutes ; the face came back again to his mind and haunted him. He could not escape from it. He was more than ever determined that he would not go home ; he dared not spend a night in the next room to it. Already the afternoon was closing in, and Bill had no notion where he was to go for the night. For the present he decided to make his way to the green ; he would probably meet other boys there that he knew.

The green to which he went is much frequented by the poor of the south-west. The railway skirts one side of it, and gives it an additional attraction to children. Bill was tired out with walking. He flung himself down on the grass to rest. His exhaustion at last overcame his fears, and he fell asleep. He slept for a long time, and in his sleep he had a dream.

It was, so it seemed to him in his dream, late in the
evening, and he was standing outside the door of the basement flat. He had knocked, and was waiting to be admitted.
Suddenly he noticed that the door was just ajar. He
pushed it open and entered. He called, but there was no
answer. All was dark. The outer door swung to with a
bang behind him. He thought that he would wait in the
kitchen by the light of the fire until some one came. He
felt his way to the kitchen and sat down in front of the fire.

It had burnt very low, and the furniture was only just dis-
tinguishable by the light of it. As he was waiting he heard
very faintly the sound of breathing. It did not frighten
him ; but he could not understand it, because as far as he
could see there was no living thing in the room except
himself. He thought that he would strike a light and
discover what it was. The matches were in a cupboard on
the right-hand side of the fireplace. He could only just
reach the fastening, and it took him some little time to undo
it. The moment the fastening was undone the door flew
open, and something yellowish-white fell or rather leapt out
upon him, fixing little quickly-moving fingers in his hair.
With a scream he fell to the floor. He had shut his eyes
in horror, but he felt compelled to open them again to see
what this thing was that clung to him, writhing and panting.
A little spurt of flame had shot up, and showed him the
face. Its eyes were blinking and rolling. Its mouth moved
horribly and convulsively, and there was foam on the white
lips. The face was close to his own ; it drew nearer ; it
touched him. It was wet.

Bill suddenly woke and sprang to his feet, shivering and
maddened with terror. The green was dark and deserted.

A cold, strong wind had sprung up, and he heard it howling dismally. An impulse seized him to run—to run for his life. For a moment he hesitated; and then, under the shadow of the wall, slinking along in the darkness, he saw something white coming towards him, and with a quick gasp he turned and ran. He paid no heed to the direction in which he was going; he dared not look behind, for he felt sure that the nameless horror was behind him; he ran until he was breathless, and then walked a few paces, and ran again. As he crossed the road on the outer edge of the green, a policeman stopped and looked at him suspiciously. Bill did not even see the policeman. His one idea was escape.

It happened that he ran in the direction of the river. He had left the road now, and was following a muddy track that led through some grimy, desolate market-gardens. All around him there was horror. It screamed in the screaming wind with a voice that was half human; it took shape in the darkness, and lean, white arms, convulsively active, seemed to be snatching at him as he passed; the pattering of blown leaves was changed by it into the pattering of something ghastly, coming very quickly after him. For one second he paused on the river's brink; and then, pressing both his hands tightly over his eyes, he flung himself into the water.

And the river went on unconcerned, and the laws of Nature did not deviate from their regular course. So the boy was drowned. It was a pity; for he was in some ways a lovable boy, and there were possibilities in him.

*　　*　　*　　*　　*

Bill's aunt was putting the untidy bedroom straight when

his mother, opening her eyes and turning a little on the
bed, said, in a low, tired voice—

"I want Bill. Wheer's Bill?"

"I sent 'im out, dearie; 'e'll be back d'rectly. Don't
you worry yourself about Bill. Why, that drattid lamp's
a-shinin' strite onto your eyes. I'll turn it down."

There was a moment's pause, while the vehement woman
—quiet enough now—arranged the lamp and took her place
by the bedside. She smoothed the young mother's faded
hair with one hand. "Go to sleep, dearie," she said.

Then she began to sing in a hushed, quavering voice.
It was a favourite hymn, and for devotional purposes she
rarely used more than one vowel-sound—

"Urbud wuth me! Fust fulls thur uvvun-tud."

THE GIRL AND THE BEETLE.

A STORY OF HERE AND HEREAFTER.

O N the brushwood and groups of trees that here and there broke the monotony of the flat and sandy common were the marks of autumn. The wind was soft and mild, and the leaves fell gently, and the white clouds sailed away into the distance steadily and unquestioningly. Far off the glint of sunlight fell on the narrow, sluggish river. Winds and leaves, clouds and river—all were going home, with a calm meekness that aggravated the dying beetle. It was a good day to die on, and the beetle knew it; but yet he was dissatisfied.

Above him there hovered two unkempt birds, tormented by a sense of what in all the circumstances was the correct thing to do. Each bird had sighted the beetle, and neither would come and take it; for each thought that the other would suppose him to be greedy. Of these two birds the one was magnanimous and the other was nervous, and both were hungry.

"There's a large beetle down there," the first remarked, "but I don't know that I care about it particularly. Won't you take it?"

There was nothing that his companion would have liked

better, but his unfortunate nervousness prevented him from
availing himself of the generous offer. " No, thanks " he
stammered, " I couldn't deprive you."

" But I really don't want it," said Magnanimity.

" Nor do I," replied Nervousness. " Let's go for a little
fly."

So they flew slowly away, feeling empty and mistaken,
with a sense that the world must be out of joint where
there were nearly always two birds to one beetle, and both
the birds understood etiquette. And the beetle went on
dying.

He had not during his previous life been a good beetle.
He was strongly built, and his constitution, which had now
given way, had always been considered robust. Female
beetles had thought him uncommonly handsome ; yet with
all these gifts he had not been a good beetle; on the
contrary he had been extremely immoral. He lay stretched
on the sand by the edge of the pathway, enjoying the
warmth of the afternoon sunlight.

" Mary," he called, a little querulously, " come out."

It is difficult to understand how the beetle could call
without making any noise. It should be remembered,
however, that sound is to beetles very much what silence
is to us. A certain kind of silence, on the other hand,
answers to what we call conversation, and can be varied
so as to express all that we can do by changing the tone
of the voice. The small female of depressed appearance,
who hurried from the shelter of a stone in answer to this
summons, quite understood that she had been called
querulously. The two unkempt birds should undoubtedly
have waited.

"Thomas," said the beetle who had been addressed as Mary, "I think you called me?"

"Have you stopped crying?"

"Yes, dear; I won't cry any more, if you don't like it."

"You know I don't like it. Have you got any new ideas?"

"Well, Thomas, nothing that could be absolutely called new, perhaps; but I remember a little story that my poor dear mother used to—— "

"Stop!" said Thomas, "you're a stale, heavy-minded female, and you can get back under the stone. I was going to let you see me die. I shan't now!"

"Do let me stop!" pleaded Mary.

"No, I won't!—stay, what's that pestilential insect creeping towards us?"

"It's the Dear Friend. He looks small and meagre, but we must not judge from looks, Thomas. Beauty fades."

Thomas surveyed Mary slowly. "It does," he said.

The Dear Friend was so named from his habit of calling indiscriminately on other beetles, and excusing himself on the ground that he wanted to be their dear friend. He lived a very good life, and he wanted other beetles to be good. The want was noble, but he had not sufficient tact to conceal it. Some beetles thought him a bore, and did not care to hear him discuss their sins in his plain way. Others, seeing that he knew so little about this life, thought that he might have unusual knowledge of the next. Beetles, as a class, have a tendency towards mysticism. Mary had a firm belief in the goodness and spirituality of the Dear Friend, although she was dimly conscious that he was not clever. She was very anxious that he should have a few words with the dying Thomas.

"You will see him, dear, won't you?" she said. "You're drawing near to your end, you know, and it would do you good to experience a word in season. You have been such a bad beetle."

"I have," said Thomas, with a chuckle of intense self-satisfaction, "I've been a devilish bad beetle."

The thought of his own exceeding immorality seemed quite to have restored his good temper. "Heavy-minded female, you are become brilliant. Never before have I experienced a word in season. You may stop, and we'll interview the Dear Friend."

Mary, like some females of higher organisations, was rarely able to understand the precise value of a satirical silence. Everything was cloudy in her brain, and nothing precise. She had vague ideas that she ought to be good, and that served her for aspirations. She had at least three decided opinions—that her mother had been very good and very kind to her, that Thomas was horribly bad and very unkind to her, and that of the two she infinitely preferred Thomas. She was emotional and rather self-seeking. At present she was very pleased at being praised, and welcomed the little visitor kindly as he crept across towards them. They formed an extraordinary trio even for beetles. It is not generally known that the lower the physical organisation the more complicated is the character. A beetle is as a rule much more contrary and difficult than a man. The character of a tubercular bacillus is so complex as to absolutely defy analysis.

"Mr. Thomas," the Dear Friend began solemnly, "I am

pleased to see you—in fact, I have come a long way with that intention. I had heard that you were very ill and like to die, and I had also heard—you will excuse me—of your past life."

"Quite right," said Thomas encouragingly, "I am guilty of having had a past life. Oh, sir, you can't think how many beetles of my age have had a past of some kind or other. It is true that it was my own life—I have not taken anyone else's, not yet—but still I've had it. I feel that deeply."

At this the Dear Friend warmed to his work, but made a fatal mistake—he grew slightly enthusiastic. Now Thomas could stand no manner of enthusiasm, because it always seemed to him to show an exaggerated conception of the value of things.

"Oh, Mr. Thomas, I am so very glad to hear you talk like that. This is indeed no time for idle compliments, and you recognise the fact. You have the sense of guilt. You see how disgusting, and loathsome, and abominable the whole of your life has——"

Here he was interrupted by a curious stridulating noise which Thomas made, thereby rendering it impossible to catch the remainder of the Dear Friend's silence. The poor little insect cooled down again at once. He saw that enthusiasm would not do; that he had been taking matters too fast, and that Thomas was a beetle who required to be treated with a good deal of tact. The Dear Friend himself was unable to stridulate, and had sometimes felt the want of it; but it is not a gift which belongs to every kind of beetle. Perhaps it would be as well to show some interest in the process, and then gradually to lead up to more serious subjects. He waited till the last whir had died away, and then he said:

"May I inquire how you make that noise? It is most interesting."

Thomas knew all about it.

"It is caused," he answered drily, "by the friction of a transversely striated elevation on the posterior border of the hinder coxa against the hinder margin of the acctabulum, into which it fits."

"Ah!" gasped the Dear Friend; but he speedily recovered himself. "That is indeed interesting—really, extremely interesting." He was trying to think in what way it would be possible to connect this with more important matters. "Talking about fits," he said, "I have just come away from such a sad case, quite a young——"

"I was not talking about fits, sir," interrupted Thomas, a little irritably. The Dear Friend hastened to agree with him.

"No, Mr. Thomas, you were not. I see what you mean, and it's very good of you to correct me. I was wrong. I was quite wrong. But you happened to use the word fits, and that suggests——"

"And talking about jests," retorted Thomas severely, "I don't think this is the time for them. When you're calmer, my friend, and have got over your inclination to make sport of serious subjects, you will see this. Please don't get excited; I'm not equal to it. You come to see me on my death-bed, and when I try to talk about my past life, you wax ribald, and begin to make puns that a school-girl would be ashamed of. I'm sorry for you, sir,—very sorry. Mary,

show that bug out. I want to think of my latter end, and
he interrupts me."

"Oh, dear, dear!" said the poor, well-meaning little
insect, almost whimpering, "I'm afraid I've made a very
bad beginning. I didn't intend to offend you, and I do
hope you'll make allowances. I know I'm not very clever,
and I'm very young, and I've never had any education to
speak of, because I've always been going about in my
humble way trying to teach others. But I do want to
be your really dear friend, and my heart does yearn
to——"

"Mary," said the exasperated Thomas, "I asked you to
show that bug out. Will you kindly go away, sir, and
drown yourself? I insist upon thinking of my latter end,
and I simply cannot do it when you are here."

"I will go away, if you wish it, Mr. Thomas, but you will
let me come back this evening?"

"You won't be able to come back, if you drown
yourself."

"But I'm not going to drown myself."

"Well, you said you were, and you ought to, any way."

"Oh, Mr. Thomas, I never, never——"

"Don't contradict. It's excessively rude, especially in a
young bug like yourself. You promised to drown yourself,
if I'd bequeath Mary to you in my will. You can take her
now, if you like, and you may both go away and drown
yourselves. I shall be dead before this evening; and if
I am quite dead, you may come back. Now go."

The Dear Friend turned slowly and sadly away.

"Are you going to take Mary?" Thomas called after
him. "You can if you like. She's nearly as fat-headed as

yourself, and you'd get on splendidly together. Pray take
her. I'm nearly dead, and I don't want her."

The Dear Friend made no reply. The wretched Mary
was crying again. Thomas had worked himself up to
the climax of fury, and was now lapsing from it into a
series of chuckles. "Moist one," he said, turning to
Mary, "you don't love me."

"Indeed I do," sobbed Mary. "I love you ever so
much too well—but you're so cruel—and you make fun
of a good cause—and you're going to die."

"Let us," said Thomas, drily, "be categorical. You,
like most other females, say too much at once. Your
remarks must be sifted and answered categorically. Firstly,
you state that you love me. Yet you display a lot of wet,
horrible emotion, in order to hasten my end. Don't speak ;
you know you did ;—and you asked the Dear Friend to come
and bore me in my last moments ; and you refused to sit on
his head, or show him out, or stop him in any way. Consequently I had to stop him myself. I had to be almost rude
to him. Perhaps you'd better go after him if you're so
fond of him. He's only half way across the path, and
you'll be able to catch him up."

"Oh, Thomas ! I'm sure I never——"

"*Will* you keep quiet ? Can't you see that I'm being
categorical ? Secondly, you say that I'm cruel. I am,
and it's not my fault. If you and other people were not
so abominably heavy-minded, I should not be cruel. You
provoke me. You needn't tell me that you can't help
being heavy-minded. I know that, and I never said that
it was your fault ; but it certainly isn't mine. Nothing that
I know of ever is anybody's fault. Thirdly, you said that I

made fun of a good cause. You muddler! I love most causes, and hate most of their promoters. Most causes are noble, and most promoters are presumptuous. So far from making fun of the good cause, I did it the greatest service by asking the Dear Friend to seek an early death. That reminds me—you said that I was going to die. So I am, if you don't mind waiting ten minutes. Why this unseemly haste?"

At this point Mary became all tears and disclaimers. "If you do that," said Thomas, "you really will have to go. I am about to die, and I intend to die my own way, without any weeping females or dear friends. It's much the same with you that it is with man and the other lower organisms. The good heart generally goes with a bad head; and if you have a good head, you probably—there, I thought so. Do you see? The Dear Friend on the further side of the path has just been trodden on by a passing labourer. If he'd had a little more head, he would have kept out of the way, and then he would not have died. Intellect is practical: spirituality is not. Now that is very curious, for although I have always been a most practical beetle, I have frequently had strong spiritual desires. For instance, I often after supper yearn to leave this gross and uncomely world, and bask in an impossible hereafter."

"Ah!" cried Mary. (She liked the ring of his last sentence.) "Those are beautiful words. If only you would always talk like that, instead of insulting those who only come to do you good. I know the Dear Friend made you angry; but then it's not so much what he said as what he wanted to say that we must think of."

"Ah, yes, my dear Mary, most moist and muddle-headed, and it is not so much what I am as what I want to be that the deceased bug should have considered. You were born with a wrong head, and so you form wrong judgments. It's not your fault; nothing's anybody's fault. The Dear Friend was good, but it doesn't matter. I am bad, and that doesn't matter either. Nothing matters, and I can't understand anything, and I want to die."

Thomas threw himself on his back and kicked petulantly. Mary entreated him not to give way to temper; however, he declared that he was doing no such thing : that he was trying to think very fast, and that the action of kicking made it possible to think faster. Suddenly he stopped, and recovered his normal position. "Mary," he said, "it is clear to me, and I will make it clear to you, that nothing matters. Suppose something had an optical delusion, and the optical delusion died, and had a ghost——"

"But it couldn't, Thomas."

"I know that. I am only asking you to suppose it—and the ghost went to sleep, and dreamed that he was dreaming, that he was dreaming——"

"Oh, don't go on ! you'll only make your poor head ache ! "

"Do you think the something would care very much what happened in its optical delusion's ghost's dream's dream's dream? Yet the innermost of the three dreams would seem to be perfectly real, and the apparent reality would be due to part of the previous experience of the something, which would be filtered—or, rather, reflected—through the whole series."

"That will do. Please don't go on. I don't understand a word of it, and it's no use. Oh, *do* let us talk good."

"You are going to understand it, fat-headed one. You think that you exist; that everything is real. How do you know that it is so? When you dream, you imagine that the dream is quite real; but you wake up and find that you are wrong. Now suppose the something one day had a thought, that went through a million optical delusions, a billion ghosts, and a trillion dreams——"

"It's not a bit of good," interpolated Mary. "I can't imagine numbers like that."

"That thought might ultimately take the form of this world, of which I, Thomas, the beetle, am a considerable part. There is nothing impossible about that. It may be so, and I am inclined to think that it is so, because something inside me seems to be struggling to get back to its origin. But if it is so it must be perfectly clear to you that nothing matters, because nothing is real, and nothing will be real till it gets back again to the—the something!"

"I don't understand it," said Mary; "are you quite sure that it doesn't confuse you at all to think that way?"

"Absolutely sure," said Thomas, which was untrue.

"And how do you get back again to the something?"

"That," said Thomas drily, "I will show you in a few minutes if, as I said before, you do not mind waiting."

For a short time neither of them spoke. The sun, like the spoiled child who promises to be so good if you will only let him stop, was growing more beautiful than ever as the time drew near for his departure. He had nothing but vapour and light with which to work, and yet he produced some very pretty effects. The gravel path, near which Thomas and Mary were lying, led into the road which skirted the edge of the common; along this road was a line of detached villas. The sun did the best that he could with them, but felt that he could not do much. The last house in the line was much larger than the rest, and stood in much larger grounds. The advertisement had described them as being park-like, and they certainly contained quite enough trees almost to hide the house from the views of those who passed on the road. The sun had found out one of the windows through the foliage and was making it blaze. He liked doing that. He could see a good deal of the house and grounds ; in point of height he had the advantage of passers-by. He could see two tennis-courts, the players, groups who had gathered to look on, others who strayed aimlessly about and tried to prove they were not suburban. It was all cup and conversation, and it rather bored the sun, who has a masculine mind. None of the people in that garden were aware that rather less than half a mile from the house a remarkably fine beetle was dying in his sins ; if they had known it, they might possibly not have cared.

When Thomas began to talk again, he appeared to be continuing a line of thought of which he had not considered it worth while to give the beginning.

" So the truth of the matter is that a beetle did once get there—right up beyond the stars, but he never carried a man there. Aristophanes said he did, but that was an ætiological myth. He made up the story to account for a prevalent belief that man could rise to higher things."

" That was what the Dear Friend always said," murmured Mary reflectively. " Cows, and pigs, and men, and fowls can never get up there—only beetles. It's all kept for them."

" And it's not what I say," retorted Thomas sharply. " I've

got better things to do in my last moments than to waste them in agreeing with anybody. The mistake the man made was not in supposing that he could rise. All beasts can rise, as much as we can. His mistake was in rejecting the supernatural, and thinking that he could be raised only by a beetle. We may have more spirituality than men. That is quite possible : they are a lower organism. We may perhaps find it easier to soar than they do. But I am sure that all are going there, just as we are, beyond the stars."

"'That may be true," said Mary, plucking up a little spirit ; " but it certainly was not the opinion of the Dear Friend. Only beetles can rise."

" Do you prefer the opinions of the Dear Friend to absolute truth ? "

" I do," said Mary proudly.

" Oh, blind and fat of temperament ! " [This does not read quite right, but it is a fairly literal translation. There are no polite English words that exactly express the silence which Thomas used on this occasion.] " A few days ago I was down in the grass by the river. It looks sweet and green from here. It grows long, and it makes a pleasant shade above one ; but at the roots it's all mud and muck. That is the way of the world; instead of grumbling at the mud we might just as well be thankful for the grass; however, that's not my point. The cows came down to drink while I was there. They are nasty, lumpy animals; you can see their slobbering mouths and great yellow teeth as they bend over one to crop the grass. Some beetles get nervous, but I don't fancy there's any danger. As one of those brutes stooped down, I looked up and saw right into its eyes. It was like looking into immeasurable distance.

They were sad, humble, trustful eyes; but there was something in them which signified the consciousness of a purpose in being. That is my point. A poor devil of a cow! it couldn't have told any one why it existed, it could not even have put the reason clearly in its own mind; but it *knew*. I am much like the beast. I know, but I cannot say, not even to myself, the reason for my existence. Sometimes I think that if all sounds were in my power, I could get the whole thing out in music. It is a thing which defies ordinary processes and all logical connexion. I see the fading sunlight writing something on the under edge of a cloud; the intellectual part of me cannot read that language, but something else in me reads it, and understands it, and answers it almost piteously. 'Oh that I might fly away and be at rest!' And suddenly the conviction is strong in me that I know why I am here, and what I shall be hereafter. In the awful silence of the night that conviction comes dropping down my dark mind like a falling star. In moments of acute dyspepsia I always feel it."

He grinned pleasantly. He had spoiled his own poetry, and that pleased him. In his former life he had always been trying to make pretty things, and had always broken them up again. The grin passed from him, and he continued:

"Cows, therefore, have souls. You needn't contradict me, and thrust that omniscient Dear Friend down my throat, because I won't stand it. I tell you that I saw into their eyes, and I know. If you want to get at the bottom of things, you must leave all ordinary processes, all logical processes. You can't crawl down that way: you must jump. The people who dare not jump see that you have got to the bottom of things, and comfort themselves with saying that you must have hurt your poor head terribly. Have I hurt my head, Mary? For my intellect is all gone, and the light is fading very quickly. You hate men, I think. Never despise them any more; for they have souls. They cut down the grass, and it dies. They pull the flowers, and they die. They tread on the beetles, and they die. They kill the animals, cut down the trees, and poison the rivers. Where a man comes, death always follows. They are murderers; they are hideously ugly; they make unpleasant noises, and do not understand silences; they are the very lowest of all creatures, but they are on their way to a hereafter. Nothing's wasted: the very strictest economy is practised."

"I can't understand you, Thomas; and I am afraid that you are getting worse. It tries you to talk. Why did you say the light was fading? The sun is still shining all over us. Oh, Thomas, you'll be gone soon—may I cry now? I must."

Thomas did not seem to have heard her. "I have been wicked, and yet not I," he said. "It was something bad in me that will pass. And the world did provoke me terribly; it would be so emotional and stupid."

Mary was crying unreservedly, but Thomas did not notice it.

"Something," he said, "has come into my head which wants thinking out, but I will not bother myself. I have the easier way. Good-bye—for the sake of old times— Mary, darling. I am going to know everything."

Then he curled up his legs quietly, and died.

Mary stopped crying, and examined the body. Yes, he was quite dead. Then she started away on a journey.

Thomas had been a wicked beetle, and he had talked wrongly in his last moments, and she was afraid to be near his body. Besides, she had heard of a vacancy.

The sun had quite finished with the window of that villa now, and the park-like grounds were nearly empty. On one of the courts a few enthusiasts were still playing, and would continue to play until they went in to dress. Out through the gate a young man sauntered into the road. The look of an escaped animal was on his face. He had been talking to a number of people whom he neither knew nor wanted to know. He had seen nothing of Marjorie, his host's daughter, a child who always pleased and generally amused him. He felt that he had done much for his hostess ; he had suffered privations. And now he was glad that the bulk of the visitors—all who were not staying in the house—had gone. He took the path across the common, pausing to light a pipe with a wax match and an air of relief. He walked in the direction of the spot where the dead body of Thomas was lying.

One of the two unkempt birds came slowly flying back again. It was he to whom the surname of Magnanimity has been given. He had got rid of his companion by some pretext of an appointment, and he had come back again to look for that beetle. He swooped down close beside the dead body of the insect, and turned it over with his beak.

" That's just my luck," he murmured softly. " I never could stand cold meat." But that was affectation.

At this moment a small stone struck the ground within a foot of where the unkempt bird was standing. He hopped away in an aggrieved fashion.

"I won't fly away yet," he said sulkily, " it would only

make the man conceited. They're always chucking stones, these fools of men, and they hardly ever hit anything. They like to think that we're afraid of them, and I'm not the least bit afraid."

Another stone missed by a sixteenth of an inch the bird's tail-feathers, and Magnanimity with one scream of bad language flew upwards. When he got there, he found that his nervous and unkempt companion had come back again, and had been watching him all the time. Then the magnanimous fowl swore worse than ever. There was no doubt that the nervous one would have a pretty story to tell about that pretended appointment.

The young man, who had thrown the stones, sauntered slowly up and surveyed the dead beetle, taking it in his hand to examine it more closely. He knew something about beetles—he had collected them in his school-days— and he saw that this was a large one of its kind, a fine specimen. He slipped it into one of his coat pockets, and strolled slowly back again to the house. He had originally meant to go further, but he had changed his intention. He was comparing in his own mind his favourite Marjorie, a child not quite fifteen, with the finished and ordinary girl as turned out in large numbers for the purposes of suburban tennis. He was also wondering casually why there were any beetles in the world, and why he had once been so interested in them.

When he got back to the house he paused in the hall for a second, and then went slowly upstairs to a room at the top of the house, used as a schoolroom by Marjorie and her governess, Miss Dean.

Marjorie was seated at the table writing. She had a

large French dictionary by her side. She was dressed in dark blue serge. Her long hair had become a little untidy in her struggle to be idiomatic. She had a pale, intelligent face. She looked up as the young man entered.

"I'm awfully glad you've come," she said, smiling. "It was getting rather dull, being all alone. Did you have some good setts?"

"No, not particularly—didn't play much. I talked, and made myself useful, and ate ices, and drank things most of the time. You can't see like that." He struck a match, and lit the gas, and then he seated himself at the piano. "Where's Miss Dean?"

"Oh, she went away as usual at half-past five, and left me this stuff to do for to-morrow. I'm doing it now, because I am going to be down in the drawing-room to-night. Only three more days to the holidays!"

"Have you got any tea?"

Marjorie nodded her head towards a table at the side of the room. "They brought it up about an hour ago," she said. "It's quite cold—will you ring for some more?"

"No, thanks," he answered, as he got up and helped himself. "This will do very well. I am not really thirsty, because, as I said, I have been drinking during the whole of the afternoon—more or less. But I never feel absolutely sociable unless I am either smoking or drinking. Have you got much more to do for the estimable one?"

"Oh, no, only a few words. It was a shorter bit than usual, and I expected to have got it finished ever so long ago. But when it came to doing it, there were a lot of words that I'd never seen before. I know the French for a plate, or a glass, or a horse, or a hat, or anything like that.

But I always have to look up words like buttercup or grid-iron. Now here's a word of that kind. What's the French for beetle?"

"Escarbot, I believe, but I wouldn't swear to it."

"Look here, Maurice," Marjorie said very earnestly, leaning her pretty little chin on one hand, "I'll tell you what I've noticed. When a thing's different in one way, it's always different in another. If a piece for translation is extra short, there are always more words to look up. If I have an awfully bad morning, and Miss Dean is savage, and Aunt Julia patronises me, and Miss Matthieson makes me kiss her—bah!—I'm always glad at the end of it, because I know I am going to have a specially good afternoon or evening."

"Marjorie, I believe you're right. You'll have a bad morning to-morrow if that wretched piece about the grid-irons and beetles isn't done for the inestimable Dean."

"Well, I'll finish in less than two minutes. Play something while I'm doing it."

He opened the piano and took down the first piece that came. It was a drawing-room piece, and had the entire absence of soul which always appealed to the corresponding vacuum in the chilly Miss Dean. It was moderately difficult, and sounded *very* difficult. Miss Dean well knew that when a girl like Marjorie, not yet fifteen, played that piece properly, it would be acknowledged to reflect great credit on her teacher. Maurice Grey opened the piece, looked at it suspiciously, skipped the introduction, played a few bars from the first page, glanced at the fifth page, then shut it up, and put it back again on the top of the piano with a sigh.

" I hate that too," said Marjorie. " Play the thing you played to them last night in the drawing-room."

" You weren't in the drawing-room last night."

" No, but my bedroom's just above, and I could hear it. It went like this." She hummed a few bars.

Maurice began to play once more. It was a mischievous, tender, eccentric little dance that went laughing about the piano as if it were mad. Marjorie had finished her work, and rose from the table and stood beside him, watching him with dark, attentive eyes as he played. She was thinking that she liked Maurice. He knew the right way to treat her. Aunt Julia treated her like a baby, and other visitors often appeared to be under the impression that children like inanity. Her father was rather an apathetic man, yet he had the sincerest affection for his wife, his only daughter, and young Maurice Grey. He had many acquaintances, but no other friends. He had been " Meyner and Sons," who did great things in iron, but he disposed of his business to a company soon after his marriage. He was absorbed in the study of psychology, and made many curious experiments upon himself. In one or two of these young Maurice had been of some service to him. But in his family affections, his studies, or his experiments, he showed very little enthusiasm. He never expected to get great results. " The evidence is so bad," he said to Maurice once, speaking of his favourite pursuit. " On my subject men lie often intentionally ; and often deceive themselves and lie unintentionally, and rarely speak the truth. Also I find out more and more that I cannot even trust my own senses. The human brain is a shockingly defective instrument." He was a little sensitive, and to visitors in

his house—with the exception of Maurice—he would talk
of anything but psychology.   Psychology, he found, was
a thing they never understood at all, and at which they
generally laughed.   Marjorie's mother, Mrs. Meyner, was
not so apathetic or so pessimistic, but then her horizon
was not extended.   The circle of her friends and relations
gave her enough to think about and to make life worth
living.   She was a very gentle, unselfish woman, and had
a provoking knack of sincerely liking nearly everybody.
Her half-sister, Julia, had the opposite knack of hating
nearly everybody.   Julia was old and unmarried, and had
a wonderful tongue ; she dressed perfectly, had snowy hair,
a kind face, a sweet smile, gentle ways, and a perfectly
venomous disposition.   Marjorie did not like her Aunt
Julia.   She did not like Miss Matthieson much better—a
sentimental woman.   Miss Dean was too chilly a person
to like exactly ; Marjorie respected her sometimes.   But
she did like Maurice, and she liked the music that he was
playing now.

"That is awfully nice," she said, when the piece was
finished.   "What is it?"

Marjorie's aunt Julia had asked the same question of
him the night before in the drawing-room, and he had told
her that the piece was by Grieg, which was untrue, and
which he knew to be untrue.   He was not aware that that
cheerful, spiteful, and horribly intellectual old lady also
knew that he was lying.   He had felt it better to blaspheme
the name of Grieg than to give her a chance by owning
that he had composed the thing himself.   He was a young
man of dangerously diverse talents.   He was just at the
end of his first year at Cambridge, and was reading for the

Classical Tripos. Now the Classical Tripos is a jealous mistress, and admits of no rivals. Nevertheless, he had become a very fair oar, was socially popular, and had devoted much time to psychology and more to music. The end of such a course is generally failure. He did not mind telling Marjorie about the little dance he had just been playing.

" Well," he said, " I have a general impression that it is mine ; but there's a touch of Grieg about it. In fact, I risked telling your aunt Julia last night that it was Grieg's. I daren't tell her it was mine."

"Yes," said Marjorie sadly, "she is awful. She pats me gently on the head, and tells me I'm a good little child, and that I may run away to the nursery and play. It's perfectly maddening. She knows as well as I do that I'm nearly fifteen, and that it's absolute nonsense to talk like that. She does it on purpose to make me angry, and I hate being angry."

Maurice took a long sip at his cold tea.

" Yes," he said, " the people in this world want sorting. Have you finished your piece about the beetle and the gridirons ? "

"Oh, yes ! There's nothing in it really about gridirons, but a beetle comes into it—a dead beetle—— "

" By Jove ! " said Maurice suddenly, thrusting his hand into his pocket, " that reminds me ! " He pulled out the dead body of Thomas, and laid it carefully on the table.

" There," he said, " what do you think of that ? "

" It's perfectly horrible," said Marjorie. " Where did you get it ? What did you do it for ? "

" I strolled on to the common after tennis for a smoke,

and I happened to find it. I used to collect these things when I was at school. I suppose I picked it up from force of habit, but I'm sure I don't know. You ought not to call it horrible, you know. It's really a fine specimen of its kind."

Marjorie looked at it more closely, turning it over with the end of a penholder.

"Do you remember saying just now," said Maurice, "that things which were different in one way were generally different in another? Beetles are different from us; they can't do the same things; we despise them; they haven't as good a time. Perhaps they can do things we don't know anything about; perhaps they despise us; perhaps they are going to have a better time in some other world. What are all the stars for?"

Marjorie wrinkled her brows, and kicked one tiny slipper half off.

"I almost think I see what you mean——"

"I am not at all sure I meant anything," said Maurice. "It was just a suggestion."

Marjorie had thrown down the penholder, and taken the body of Thomas in her hand.

"Beetles might have some secrets that we know nothing about. But Miss Dean says that all insects were sent into the world for the birds to eat."

Maurice was silent for a moment. He was remembering that Miss Dean had remarked to him the day before that she considered that the birds had been created to kill the insects. "I should like to talk the question over with a beetle. Now I must be off and dress."

When he had gone an old trick of Marjorie's younger

days came back to her. She had often, in her babyhood, held conversations with voiceless or inarticulate things, such as dolls or cats, and on one occasion, after a stormy music lesson, she had made the piano promise to *make* the music come out right next time. She had always to do the speaking for them, so it was not quite convincing; but it was helpful and consolatory in its way. And now she began to talk to the beetle aloud, holding it on the palm of one little white hand—

" Beetle, tell me your secrets. Tell me all your secrets."

There was silence.

"I want to know if beetles are as good as men. Are they? Are they better than men? Are there better things than we ever think of doing, which we might do if it was only possible to think of them? *Do* tell me. I won't tell anybody, except Maurice and mamma, if she asks me, but she won't. You *might* tell me—it's quite safe."

There was only silence; but then it has been proved already that silence is a beetle's method of speech. Perhaps the spirit of Thomas was there and answered her; perhaps it was elsewhere; perhaps Thomas never had a spirit.

Marjorie put the beetle down again on the table, with a laugh at herself for her silliness.

In the drawing-room that night, she saw very little of Maurice. Aunt Julia looked as perfect and sweet and gentle an old lady as ever; and her conversation was just as poisonous as usual. Her temper must even have been a little worse than normal. She commenced to talk about psychology with Mr. Meyner, because she knew that he hated discussing it with the uninitiated. She insisted that he was joking—the poor man never joked; he was half earnestness and half apathy—and she told him untrue stories. When he escaped, she fastened on to Miss Matthieson, who was a sentimental and ignorant woman, with a desire to love art. She invented an entirely fictitious picture of Turner, described it, and gave its precise position in the National Gallery ; she finally made Miss Matthieson talk about it, become enraptured about it, and confess what her sensations were when she first saw it. She did not enlighten her ; that would have been too crude an enjoyment for Aunt Julia. Her smile became just a little sweeter, and she assured Miss Matthieson that she had learned much from her. Maurice Grey had, for reasons of his own, been playing Chopin's Funeral March. " And is that also by Grieg ? " she asked him, looking interested.

" No, it is not," he said shortly. He knew very well that Aunt Julia knew very well what he had been playing; and he saw what she meant by her question.

" Oh, please don't be angry with me," she said. " I'm no musician, you know, Mr. Grey,"—her knowledge of music was, as Maurice was aware, considerably above the average—" and I make stupid mistakes. Last night you played a little dance which you told me was by Grieg. Now, I never should have known it; I thought it was pretty enough, but just a little weak and—well, almost amateurish, you know. You played it again in the school-room this afternoon, and you altered the last part of it. What *is* that thing you played just now ? "

" Chopin's Funeral March."

" Are you going to make any—any improvements in it, as you did in the Grieg ? And why did you play a funeral march ? I suppose the sight of an old woman like myself, among so many young people, suggested the thought of death. Ah, yes—very natural."

This was absolutely intolerable, but Maurice was not allowed to protest or escape.

" It is a great mistake," said Aunt Julia, earnestly, " to give one's self up to trivialities. We must all die. It is always better to think about death, even in the drawing-room after dinner. I mean that it's better for the aged, like myself. To the young it might perhaps seem a little gloomy and morbid, but I like it—I enjoy it. I shall be going to bed directly. Won't you play a few hymn tunes, Mr. Grey, before I go? You might play the Dies Iræ."

She did not go to bed until she had maddened about half the people in the room. Even Mrs. Meyner found it difficult at times to make excuses for Aunt Julia. Maurice Grey managed to be moderately polite to her as a rule ; he generally shammed stupidity, and refused to see the point of any of her sarcasms. He found afterwards that this style of treatment had impressed Miss Julia Stone. When Marjorie came round to say good-night to Maurice, she spoke to him about the beetle.

" Do you want that dead beetle ? " she asked. " Shall I keep it for you ? "

" Yes, keep it."

" Are you going on collecting again then ? "

" No, I don't think so—but it is too good a specimen to throw away just anywhere. How would you like to be thrown away ? "

" It's not quite the same thing, you know, Maurice. I'm more important. But we'll treat this beetle very well—you've just played a funeral march for it—and then, perhaps, its ghost will come and tell us all about beetles, and what beetles think about men, and if they know anything that we don't."

"Yes, treat it kindly," said Maurice, smiling. "Much can always be done by kindness."

Marjorie went out of the room laughing; but on the following morning, when she appeared at breakfast, she was very quiet and subdued. A note came from Miss Dean, regretting that—"owing to a slight indisposition"—she was unable to come to teach Marjorie that morning. Even the prospect of a day's holiday did not seem to cheer her up. Maurice found her alone in the garden about an hour afterwards.

"What's up, Marjorie?" he said. "Aren't you well?"

"Oh, yes, I'm always well—I've got something to tell you though. I saw it last night."

"Saw what?"

"The beetle."

Maurice was a little startled. He too had had a curious dream in which the beetle had figured. "Look here, Marjorie," he said; "I've nothing particular to do this morning, and I believe you'd be the better for a walk. We'll go over to Weyford, and then go up to St. Margaret's, if you don't mind climbing the hill."

"Oh, that would be lovely! That's just the thing. We shan't get back to lunch, you know."

"That's all right. We'll lunch in Weyford. I'll go in and talk to Mrs. Meyner about it, and you go and get ready."

The morning sunlight and the cool wind made walking pleasant. That unkempt bird, whom we have called

Magnanimity, was taking out quite a young bird for a little exercise. They saw Maurice and Marjorie walking together.

"Those are men," said the young bird. "Bless your heart—I've seen lots of 'em."

"Just drop that," said Magnanimity, sternly. "There's nothing more sickening than to hear a mere chick like yourself setting up to be a complete bird of the world. Fancy taking any notice of contemptible, ugly men!"

"That young she-man," said the mere chick, "isn't at all ugly. I often wish I were a man."

"You'd soon wish you were a bird again," retorted Magnanimity. "Are you aware that men can't fly, or lay eggs, or talk our language, or do anything really worth doing? Are you aware that we old birds lead them the very devil of a life?"

"How do you do it?" asked the mere chick, quite unable to keep the wonder and admiration out of the tone of its voice.

"Why, we mock at 'em—sneer at 'em till they can't bear themselves."

Marjorie and Maurice walked on, talking of indifferent things. They climbed the hill, resting occasionally in the shade of the plantations that grew on its sides. They reached the summit at last, a solitary place where the ruined chapel of St. Margaret stood in a little deserted grave-yard. The wind was fresh and cool. They could see far away into the distance; they could see the river winding along down the valley, until it was a mere thread of silver; they could see the smoke curling up from low, red-roofed cottages and farm-buildings, scattered here and there.

Maurice stretched himself at full length on the grass, and endeavoured to light a cigarette. There was just enough wind to blow a match out. There always is.

"Now then, Marjorie, you had a dream last night."

"Yes!"

"And it frightened you."

"No—no—well, it didn't exactly frighten me—it made me think. It was all nonsense, you know, and yet it was the realest dream I ever had in my life."

"Stop a minute. You had some coffee in the drawing-room, and that kept you awake for a long time, you turned about from side to side, and thought about the beetle. Your bedroom seemed hot and stifling."

"Yes, that's all true—how did you know, Maurice?—but it has not got anything to do with it."

"Marjorie, if you'd never had that coffee, you'd have never had that dream. Now, then, let's hear it. I'll try to keep awake, but walking always makes me sleepy."

"After I had said good-night to everybody, I went up into the schoolroom and got the beetle, because I was afraid the servants might throw it away in the morning, and you said you wanted it. I took it into my own room, and put it down on a table. All the while I was undressing, I kept thinking about it and wondering if beetles and other things could really understand, or if it were only men and women who knew about things, and if all the world were just made for us alone. Before I got into bed I picked the beetle up, and said to it, 'Beetle, you've got to come into my dream to-night, and tell me all about it. Don't forget.' Of course that was just a fancy. I didn't really think it could understand what I said, or that it would

come. I'm not a baby, though Aunt Julia treats me like
one sometimes. Well, for a long time I couldn't get to
sleep, but at last I did."

"And then the beetle came and suffocated you, or threw
you over a precipice," remarked Maurice, drowsily.

"No, that's not a bit like it. I don't know how long I
had been asleep, but I dreamed that I woke up suddenly,
and that the moonlight was streaming in at the window.
Right in the middle of the moonlight was the beetle,
standing up on his hind legs. He had grown ever so much
bigger, and was as tall as I am. 'Come on, now,' he said.
'How much longer are you going to keep me waiting?
I'm late, as it is.'

"I didn't feel the least bit afraid of him. I just asked
him where we were going. He opened the window, and
pointed upwards. 'Well,' I said, you must wait till I'm
dressed, else I shall catch cold.' However, he wouldn't
wait, and so I got out of bed. We climbed up on to the
table in front of the window. 'Now then,' he said, 'you
must keep hold of my fore leg, or you'll fall.' We didn't
fly or walk ; we floated out of the window, and then upwards, going very quickly and steadily, as if a wind were
blowing us. As we were floating up, the beetle's head
changed till it became just like Aunt Julia's. 'Marjorie's
an unnatural child,' it said in Aunt Julia's voice. 'She
doesn't care for dolls—doesn't care for anything except
music and Maurice.'"

Maurice had an unworthy and needless impression that
the girl was making some of this up. He looked at her
curiously, as though he were going to say something ; but
he refrained, and she continued her dream—

"I didn't quite know what to say, but I told the beetle that he was entirely wrong—that I liked papa and mamma very much indeed, and rather liked almost everybody. Then I asked him how he managed to speak, being a beetle, and how he could hear me speak. He told me that neither of us had spoken a word : when I contradicted him, he said that if I had gone back to my own room I should have found that my real body was still lying asleep in bed. 'Now,' he pointed out, 'you can't speak without your body —so that is proved.' Then he said that beetles never spoke, and that as a matter of fact we were not speaking, but just understanding each other's silence. Still, it seemed just like speaking. We must have moved very quickly, because by this time we had got quite beyond the moon. I could see it ever so far beneath my feet, and the stars all scattered about the darkness ; yet I didn't remember passing them on our way up. I didn't feel at all cold. As the beetle went on talking—it was just like real talking, so it doesn't matter whether it was real or not—he stopped being like Aunt Julia. He got his own head back again, and his own voice—except that sometimes it began to be rather like yours. You haven't gone to sleep, have you ?"

Maurice had not gone to sleep, and said so.

"The strangest thing was that although his body had not really changed—except that it was so much bigger—it didn't seem at all ugly now. In fact, I liked to look at it, and didn't at all mind keeping hold of its fore-leg. I think the beetle must have known what I was thinking about, for all of a sudden he said, as if he were sorry for me : 'Poor Marjorie ! Poor little Marjorie ! They've taught you all wrong, and they taught me all wrong. But I had a glimpse

of the right thing: I always knew that human beings were
not half as ugly as they seemed to be. I said as much, but
it was of no use to talk to the Dear Friend. As for Mary—
that fat-headed female had believed so many other things
that she had no capacity left for believing any more. I,
however, had got plenty of room left—oh, yes, plenty of
room.' When he said that he chuckled in the most
horrible way you ever heard. 'Now I come to think of it,'
he went on, 'I believe I did *say* that the human breed
were ugly. It was such a tame thing to believe anything
that one said; it was a thing that Mary always did, and so I
didn't. Marjorie, if the good people hadn't been good, I
should have liked goodness.'"

"But who were Mary and the Dear Friend?" asked
Maurice.

"I don't know any more than you do. I don't think he
liked the Dear Friend very much; sometimes he seemed to
hate Mary, and sometimes he seemed to love her and pity
her. Now do you know what he told me? He said
positively that all beetles believed that they had souls which
never died, and that the sun, and stars, and everything were
made for them alone. They believed that men, and other
animals, had no souls at all. I told him how very absurd
that was, and tried to explain to him what was really the
case; but he only chuckled horribly again. But as we went
up higher and higher he got more grave, and he didn't
laugh any more; and once or twice he said to me quite
sadly, 'Poor little Marjorie, you are very young to bother
yourself about these things. You only know part—only
part—and I cannot tell you the rest—I may not!' I began
to get quite sorry for him, because it seemed to trouble

him; I think he really wanted to tell me some more things. Just then I saw up above us a River of Light. It was flowing very swiftly and smoothly, and looked like melted gold. I don't know why, but I wanted to plunge into the River. It seemed to be the only thing worth doing, or that ever had been worth doing. I never wanted anything so much before in my life, but the beetle would not let me go. Last of all I began to cry; I really did, and you know, Maurice, that I hardly ever cry. But it was of no use; he still kept tight hold of my hand. The darkness was all grey darkness, except one black piece which stuck up like a mountain. We stopped on the top of it, and looked down at the River. I kept on crying—I do not know why, but I think it was because it all seemed strange and awful. I may have been frightened a little, but it was not quite like being frightened. There was a long pause, and then the beetle said, 'Ah, if you only knew now, Marjorie! And if I had only known then!'

"Just then out of the grey darkness came a thread of light, like a little snake, moving very quickly and curling about as if it were glad; it hurried towards the great River of Light, and melted into it and was gone. I was eager about it, and asked the beetle what it was. 'I may tell you that,' he replied. 'It was a soul going home!' I stopped crying then; I felt something the way I feel at an evening service in a church in summer time, when they are singing one of the hymns I like best. It was a sort of quiet happiness; I can't explain it properly, but I never felt so happy as I did then. 'Beetle,' I said, 'you must tell me the rest now.'

"'I will tell you one thing,'" he said.

"What was it?" asked Maurice quickly.

For a few seconds Marjorie did not answer. There was a queer dreamy look in her eyes. At last she said,—

"Maurice, I'm afraid you'll think now that I have been making all this up, but I haven't. I can't tell you what the beetle said, because I *don't know*. It was about you, and it was very important. I don't even know whether it was good or bad. It has gone straight out of my memory, and I *can't* get it back again. I'd give anything to be able to remember it. I've been thinking about it all the morning.'

"I believe you entirely," said Maurice thoughtfully. "I have had much the same kind of thing happen to me in a dream."

He did not add that much the same thing had happened to him on the same night. "How did the dream end?" he went on.

"I awoke directly after the beetle told me that thing that I have forgotten. It was broad daylight. But when I got up, the beetle was not on the table where I had put it. I could not find it anywhere."

"You probably moved it in your sleep. Did you ever walk in your sleep?"

"Once, when I was quite little—almost a baby. I had got out into the garden, and my nurse found me there."

Maurice rose, and the two went down the hill together. "I wouldn't trouble about all that if I were you," said Maurice. "These things can generally be explained in the simplest way when one goes through them carefully. Coffee, the action of the heart, the position of the body in bed, the sounds that one hears while asleep, all help to explain a good deal, you know."

He did not tell her his own dream. He thought, perhaps rightly, that a young girl, unacquainted with the study of mathematics, might be unduly impressed by coincidences which were unusual but did not require a supernatural explanation. He did not want to frighten her, or let her grow superstitious. Yet during the day he thought a good deal about the two dreams.

He had dreamed that he was seated on the one side of the fireplace in his rooms at Cambridge, and that the beetle, with the same exaggerated dimensions with which Marjorie had seen him, was seated in a lounge chair on the other side. They were discussing Maurice's psychological studies, and Maurice was describing to him some of the curious experiments which he had made in conjunction with Mr. Meyner. Every difficulty that Maurice propounded the beetle made clear at once. He even suggested fresh problems which had not occurred to Maurice before, and was equally ready with their solution. His last words before Maurice awoke were: "There are many things besides which you ought to know, and of which you have not realised your own ignorance. You will know them all one day."

This was all that Maurice could remember of his dream. The difficulties propounded and the explanations given had passed completely out of his recollection. He was only conscious that during his dream he had felt an exhilarating sensation of having known for certain things which he had thought it impossible that anyone, at least in this life, could know at all.

Shortly afterwards he returned to Cambridge. By this time Marjorie seemed to have recovered her normal spirits.

She made no further allusion to her dream. She was
unaffectedly sorry at the departure of Maurice.

Maurice had not been long at Cambridge before he
received news of the sudden death of Mr. Meyner. Apart
from the friendship he had always felt for Mr. Meyner, the
death seemed to him peculiarly distressing and pathetic.
The man had worked hard at a study which fascinated him,
not from any desire for gain, or fame to be derived from it,
but with the most genuine devotion to the study itself; and
he had died before his work was done, before he had
arrived at any large and definite result. Yet Maurice felt
assured that Meyner's patience, and judgment, and freedom
from prejudice, would, if he had but lived longer, have
brought him some reward, some light. He had always
distrusted and undervalued himself; his humility was
genuine, but almost irritating. He had been at school, and
subsequently at college, with Maurice's guardian, and had
first met Maurice when he was a boy of fifteen; the friendship between the boy and the middle-aged man had formed
slowly, but surely, since then; yet, although he gave every
sign of his liking for Maurice, he never seemed to expect
Maurice to like him in return; he certainly never realised
the admiration which Maurice had for his knowledge and
attainments. So too he loved his wife and only child
dearly, and he knew that they loved him; but he had never
realised how much they loved him, and would very possibly
have thought such love almost irrational. To some extent,
perhaps, his studies had spoiled him; he had been groping
in the darkness after great things, and the one result that he
seemed to have found there was a sense of his own insigni-
ficance. Yet, illogically enough, he had never thought

others insignificant; he had never reached the cynical conclusion that nobody matters very much. If his friends and his sympathies were so few, it was not because the outside world did not matter to him, but because he could not believe that he mattered to the outside world. He had died without ever having learned his own value.

A parcel which was forwarded to Maurice from Mrs. Meyner shortly afterwards contained the many note-books which her husband had filled with the evidence he had collected, and the work he had done, until death interrupted him. With them was a simple and pathetic letter that he had written to Maurice on the day before he died. "Look through them," the letter said, in reference to the note books. "You will see and understand what I was aiming at. If you think it worth while, carry on the investigation which I began; I own that it is some pleasure to me to think that it is possible that you may do so; that one who was intimate with my views, and who shared some of my opinions, which are not generally held, may be able to give those views and opinions their justification. But I do not want you to pledge yourself in any way, nor do I ask you to give up your tripos or your career at college for the purpose."

Maurice paused as he read this last sentence. How often he had thought, as he turned English verse into indifferent alcaics, that this classical work could only lead, was only educative, could never be considered as an end. But he came to no final decision until he had spent nearly a month in a rapid survey of those note-books. They startled him; the minute accuracy and patience shown in the collection of evidence were only what he expected from such a man as Meyner, but the brilliant audacity of his theories,

the almost savage independence of an original mind, looked
far different when plainly stated in black and white, than
when they had fallen humbly and almost hesitatingly from
the man's own lips. The romantic side in Maurice's
character was touched most by what was worst in Meyner's
books; the finished and unprejudiced scholar would have
shaken his head over much that looked like vain imagining,
that was extravagant, and, so far, unsupported. Maurice
was younger; Meyner's fierce opposition of an accepted
view attracted him, and awoke his pugnacity. He would
linger over page after page of what seemed to him splendid
conjecture, of what might have seemed to others very
useless stuff, and say to himself: " If only one could prove
that this *is* so, instead of longing that it *may* be so!" The
air of conviction with which Meyner wrote down his own
views on his own subject gained immeasurably in Maurice's
eyes from the personal knowledge which Maurice had of
Meyner's perpetual tendency to undervalue himself, and to
distrust himself in all other matters. Even with these views
in his mind, he had expected no great results; he had been
too honest to support them with any evidence that was not
thoroughly tested. They seemed to Maurice to be the
guess of genius; the air of conviction had for him the
strange attraction of a religious, not wholly rational, faith.
He decided to abandon his University career, and to
devote his time to a further prosecution of Meyner's
investigations.

His guardian, who was also his uncle, made very little
opposition. Maurice had given so much evidence that he
was stable. He had an unusually large allowance for a
young man at Cambridge, and yet he had not run into debt.

At Cambridge the wealthy are the most in debt, because they have most credit and most temptations. As a matter of fact, Maurice never had considered the financial side of anything ; it had simply happened that he had never wanted more than he could well afford. But this weighed very much in Maurice's favour with his guardian. He felt that his nephew was a man who understood value, and could be trusted. The property to which Maurice would succeed, when he came of age, made it unnecessary for him to adopt any profession ; nor did it bring with it any of those special responsibilities for which a special training is supposed to be necessary.

Maurice, therefore, spent the next two years abroad, for the most part in Paris. He had carried with him an introduction to a physician at one of the Paris hospitals, who sympathised with him in his work, and was able to be of great assistance to him. In this man he gained a friend ; in other respects these were years, it seemed to him, of disillusion. One by one the great, beautiful theories had to go ; a tiny meagre fact would start up, a fact that meant but little to the ordinary observer, and it would be strong enough to overthrow years of work, and send the conjecture on which they were founded to some limbo for lost absurdities. He had long ago been aghast when he had tried to realise how vast is the amount of the things that no man knows. And now for "knows" he put "can know."

Mrs. Meyner and Marjorie had also been abroad, but he had seen them very seldom in those two years. Marjorie seemed to be slowly changing ; he was no longer the recipient of childish confidences. She was grave and more beautiful, perhaps, than she had been ; and she was also more quiet and reserved ; she was friendly with him, up to a limit ; she told him news, of a kind ; she sympathised with his disappointments in his work, within decent bounds. At the end of the second year, when Mrs. Meyner and Marjorie were staying for a few days in Paris, and Maurice was at last awakening to the fact that he could not expect childish confidences from one who was no longer a child, Marjorie told him some news which surprised him.

" Aunt Julia has changed very much. I like her now."

" She must certainly have changed then," said Maurice smiling.

" I don't mean," Marjorie explained, " that she is different to other people—only to mamma and myself. Her servants are in terror of her, and her tenants hate her, and so on ; but she has been really kind to me. I think she likes me. We were staying with her a few weeks ago. You'll be surprised to hear that she likes you too."

" Of course," said Maurice, " it is surprising that any one likes me, as you say."

" I don't think I said that. She told me quite suddenly once that she liked Maurice Grey, because he was the cleverest man she knew in one respect. Mamma suggested that it was because you understood her. ' No, my dear,' said Aunt Julia, ' the village people do that, because I speak plainly, and they try to pay me back again for it. He always misunderstood me. I like him. He will not do much, because he can't concentrate himself on one thing ; but I like Maurice Grey all the same.' "

Marjorie did not repeat any more of Aunt Julia's conversation ; but the old lady had gone on to say that Maurice, however, would probably concentrate himself on one person. She added, in her point-blank way, that she intended him ultimately to marry Marjorie. She did not appear to think that Marjorie, or Maurice, or Mrs. Meyner, could have a voice in the matter; the marriage was one of the things that the perverse old woman had made up her mind to arrange.

"I'm glad that dear old lady likes me," said Maurice. "I always liked her—I really did. She was full of such striking and impressive contrasts—the soft, purring voice and the ill-tempered words—her gentle, peaceful face and her fearful pugnacity. And I like her more because she has been good to you, you say."

"Did you ever," asked Marjorie, hurriedly going to another subject, "find out anything new about the intelligence of the brute creation?"

"I think I used to tell some lies about a favourite terrier of mine once, and made myself believe them. No, Marjorie, that has not been my line. It has been quite enough to find out that I and you, and all the rest of us, have got no intelligence worth mentioning, none that will do a thousandth part of what we want it to do. What made you ask that?"

"I was thinking about that beetle you found on the common when you were stopping with us once, and about the dream I had."

"Ah! I remember that."

"I never found the dead beetle, although I hunted everywhere for it, and I never remembered what it told me about you."

"I did not tell you at the time, Marjorie, but I had a dream about the beetle that same night. It came to me that night and told me everything I wanted to know—the things I have been working at for the last two years. Of course, they were all gone when I awoke, but I can remember it saying that I should know them all one day. I am afraid that dead beetle lied."

"Maurice," said Marjorie suddenly, "sometimes a thought flashes across my mind that in a minute I may be dead. I don't know even what life and death mean; yet I have to live and die. There are stars above me, but I do not know why they are there. There are beasts, and birds, and insects everywhere, and I do not know how important they are. I feel lost and horrible. No, I feel like a prisoner beating against an iron wall. For a few moments it is torture to be like that; I should kill myself or go mad if it went on. But it always passes away, and three minutes afterwards I am wondering if I will do my hair a different way——"

"Don't!" murmured Maurice, softly.

"Or I can be really angry because my maid knocks something over, or does something clumsy; when one speaks of it, it seems absurd enough. Speaking spoils everything. Lovers—in books, I mean—talk the worst nonsense, and yet that nonsense is the expression of a very fine thing. I do not think that silence is enough appreciated. I want, for instance, to let you know what I am thinking. Well, when I put the thought into words, I lose some of it, or add something to it, or I alter it by an accident with the tone of my voice. Now if I could just look at you and you at me, and we could understand one another exactly through silence, it would be splendid."

Maurice agreed with her. After two years of disappoint-

ment silence seemed to him almost the only thing left.
There was, however, one thing even more consolatory.
About a year after this conversation with Marjorie the two
met once more, and Maurice put his failures behind him
and told Marjorie that he loved her. So they both spoke
the nonsense which they deprecated. We all believe that
in affairs of the heart we are not as the others, and we are
all mistaken. With him there was an iteration of "I love
you," with a deep tremble in the voice ; and with her there
was a sighing echo of the same words, coming up between
blushes. The expression of the feeling was almost ludicrous;
the feeling itself was so sacred that the lightest touch of
thought seemed to soil it, and a writer, after turning over
his vocabulary in disgust, can find nothing explanatory
which at all matches it. But when it took place, it seemed
to Maurice the only important thing that ever had happened
to him ; the psychological studies, which had brought him
so much disappointment, appeared in a new light as a
plaything that had seemed to amuse him until love
came.

This did not happen at Paris. Maurice had returned to
England, and all of them—Mrs. Meyner, Marjorie, and
Maurice—were staying in Aunt Julia's house. It was a
lonely old house, much too big for that one wicked old
lady ; it stood outside a North Yorkshire village, just where
a grand, dignified old hill drew back its skirts, with a sharp
sweep, from contamination with human dwelling-places.
Aunt Julia owned quarries at the foot of the hill, and got
therefrom more money than was good for her. The time
was December, and the moors looked bleak and cold. But
it was a comfortable house. Aunt Julia had devoted her

many years to the study of comfort—her own comfort.
"There is nothing to shoot," she explained to Maurice,
"except my tenants down in the village. You can shoot
them, if you like. There's the library, though, which is
good, and you can smoke anywhere you like——"

" But you used to hate smoking ? " said Maurice.

" My dear Maurice, there are two of me, and you used
to know the wrong one. Down in the village they mostly
know the wrong one, and they call her, I am told, the hell-
cat, which is rude of them. Yes, you can smoke anywhere.
If you and Marjorie want to go out of the house—which is
a thing I never do in December—I believe there are some
horses round at the back. If there is anything wrong about
the horses, or Pilkin, or anything that is his, just tell me,
and I will say a word or two. I believe the man presumes
on my ignorance. You can go and see my quarries, or my
cottages ; but you had better not go to the cottages, because
they have no drains. I should like to give them some
drains, but the tenants won't let me. They are poor people,
and a strong smell makes a difference to their colourless
existence."

So Maurice did a certain amount of reading, riding, and
smoking. But, of course, Marjorie made for him the chief
charm of the house. Mrs. Meyner had willingly consented
to the engagement ; even if she had desired to oppose it,
her more strenuous half-sister would have reasoned her out
of it ; or, to use her own gentle euphemism, would have
said a word or two. The days passed quietly enough. To
Maurice they were a pleasant rest after his three years of
wasted laboriousness. " Marjorie," he said to her one
afternoon, when they had wandered over the dignified hill,

and as they came back saw the bare boughs of the trees in the plantation black against a red blot of sunset, " Marjorie, I have done with all questions. I am here, and you are here, and that is enough for me. I am going to live and love, and enjoy. Blessed be my fate that has saved me from the sordid worry of life. (Just wait a second, will you? can't get a match to light in this wind.) We will make a beautiful house, with beautiful things in it, with good books on shelves, and good wine in the cellar, and a good cook in the kitchen. And no one shall enter into that house who is not either very beautiful, or very clever, or too good for this world."

" But I shall be so lonely there without you," said Marjorie, gently, with her sparkling eyes looking groundwards.

Maurice laughed. ".Ah, Marjorie, you and I will be one, and you are more beautiful, and clever, and better than anyone in the world. That is how I shall have a right to come into my own beautiful house. We will trouble ourselves with no theories about anything. We will not get excited about anything; an excited man always has been, or will be, dull. We will make life one long, gentle enjoyment."

He spoke half in jest and half in earnest, telling his soul of beautiful things laid up in that house for many years; bidding himself to eat, and drink, and enjoy judiciously.

Perhaps it was because Marjorie at that moment looked towards the sunset. It seemed so far awa, from her, and yet so desirable. She had the fancy, common among children and poets, that the dying light looked the gate of some wonderful place to be seen hereafter.

' Maurice, Maurice !" she cried. " Look at that. I

have the lost, prisoned feeling again when I look at it. It is too far away."

That night ended all. There were beautiful things to come, so it seemed to both of them, such poetry and love as never had been before; and all was stopped by an accident, one commonplace accident, almost too poor to be put into a story.

Marjorie had been subdued, almost depressed; she had talked but little at dinner or afterwards. Mrs. Meyner and Marjorie both went to bed rather early. Maurice, restless from his love-passion, had gone to walk and smoke for an hour on the fell-side. Aunt Julia sat before the fire in the drawing-room, waiting for Maurice to return, reading a favourite chapter of Gibbon.

For some time one would have said that Marjorie was sleeping quietly and peacefully. Then suddenly she sat up in bed, her eyes still closed. She began talking in her sleep. "Tell me! Come back again and tell me. I *will* know. I am on the verge, and—and——." She stopped talking; quickly she moved from the bed to the dressing-table, and her fingers fumbled impatiently with the opening of her dressing-case. She had drawn up the blind, and the moonlight shone straight upon her. Her lips were still moving, but no sound came. She opened the dressing-case and took from it a glass jar which was filled with old dead rose leaves. She had filled it herself long before, when she was a child. She unscrewed the silver top, and began to take out the rose leaves very carefully. At the bottom of the jar she found the thing for which she had been looking, and laid it on the palm of her little white hand. It was the withered body of a large dead beetle.

For a moment she stood thus. And then she drew a long breath, and opened her eyes wide. She was awake, and she had remembered the horrible thing which she had heard in a dream and had forgotten. Quivering and almost breathless she hurried from the room, just as she was.

Aunt Julia had good nerves, but she was a little startled when the door of the drawing-room was flung open, and she saw, standing in the doorway, the figure of Marjorie, white-robed, bare-footed, with both hands stretched out, and struggling in vain, as it seemed, to speak.

" Marjorie! What is it ? " cried Aunt Julia in a shaking voice.

She found words at last.

" Maurice is dead—dead! He fell—I saw him fall— over there, against the plantation, down into the quarry. He is dead!"

There followed a burst of hysterical laughter, more bitter than any tears, and then she fainted away.

＊　　＊　　＊　　＊　　＊

Aunt Julia stood in the porch, looking out. She was white to the lips. By the moonlight she could see the procession coming nearer—two men carrying lanterns, four men carrying a hurdle with a burden upon it, covered up altogether because it was broken and ghastly.

LONDON : PRINTED BY WILLIAM CLOWES AND SONS, LIMITED, STAMFORD STREET AND CHARING CROSS.